The First to Die

Sam Kane, army scout, is a worried man, for a band of comancheros has mounted a series of successful raids on army supply trains. Is it pure chance, or is it someone at Fort Walsh supplying the bandits with valuable intelligence? Determined to find out, Sam leads a patrol deep into Comanche country in an attempt to recover a consignment of repeating rifles and to capture the renegades.

Threatened not only from without by the comancheros' roving Indian bands but also by the mysterious deaths of some of his troopers, the scout comes to realize that a killer within the patrol poses an even greater danger. But is the murderer linked to the comancheros or does he have his own agenda?

As the body count rises and Kane himself becomes a target for the silent assassin he knows he must solve the mystery, and quickly too, before the entire patrol is wiped out.

The First to Die

G. T. DUNN

A Black Horse Western

ROBERT HALE · LONDON

ISBN 0 7090 7380 1

Robert Hale Limited
Clerkenwell House
Clerkenwell Green
London EC1R 0HT

Typeset by
Derek Doyle & Associates, Liverpool.
Printed and bound in Great Britain by
Antony Rowe Limited, Wiltshire

I

Bob Bates, the sheriff of Miller Springs, looked genuinely puzzled as he stared down at the scalped and lifeless body lying in the dirt of the alleyway between the Lucky Lady saloon and Doc Stephens's office. Henry Tipper, the owner of the saloon, had found the tall, stockily built stranger lying in a pool of dried blood an hour after dawn. A low murmur arose from the small crowd gathering at the sheriff's back as the town doctor rolled the bloody corpse over on to its back, cursing under his breath. The cause of death was now plain for all to see. The wide, vivid red and blue marks around his neck showed that he had been garrotted from behind. His face had then been bashed in before, in a final orgy of violence, the perpetrator had scalped and then stripped the man down to his soiled underwear.

Miller Springs was a fairly quiet sort of place by Texan standards. The sheriff's time was usually taken up with nothing more challenging than the occasional bit of cattle-rustling or drunken cowpoke out for a good time on a Saturday night. As far as he could recall, there had only ever been three killings in the town's history, and they had all taken place on the same bloody evening almost a year to the day when three troublesome soldiers from Fort Walsh had crossed swords with a number of locals, including Bates's predecessor, Sheriff Pat Blaine. One of the innocent victims had been the young nephew of a prominent town merchant, Tom Harmer. Harmer himself had died out on the prairie at the hands of an army scout, Sam Kane, while trying to avenge the youngster's death.

'Who was he, Bob?' asked the doc, as he stood up, replacing his hat on his balding head.

'Danged if I know,' replied the young lawman, with a shrug of the shoulders. 'I doubt if his own mother would recognize him in that state!' He turned to face the stunned townsfolk. 'Can anyone throw any light on this?'

Nobody could.

'Looks like some stinking Comanch' sneaked into town last night and jumped him,' offered Henry Tipper.

'Could be,' conceded Bates, turning back to face him. 'But I ain't never heard of such a thing happening within the town limits before. A Comanch' won't normally come within a mile of a large settlement, less'n he's part of a large raiding party.'

'Nor would they cave a man's face in,' offered the doc, shaking his head.

'And why take his clothes?' offered Tipper.

'What about that half-breed scout from the fort, Curly Smith?' interjected the doc.

'What about him?'

'Well he's meaner than any full-blood Injun, and he was in town last night. I wouldn't put it past him to bushwhack anyone he took a dislike to.'

'Yeah, you're right about that,' agreed Hal Ketchum, the town carpenter, stepping forward from out of the crowd for a clearer view of the body. 'And I know fer sure the 'breed was in a foul temper last night. He came into the Lucky Lady around ten o'clock and was none too pleased when he was refused any liquor. He caused quite a scene before Henry's trusty old shotgun persuaded him to leave.'

'That's right,' confirmed the saloon-keeper.

'That's as maybe,' said Bates, 'but that don't prove he killed no one.'

'No it don't,' agreed Ketchum, 'but I still reckon you ought to check him out.'

'I will, don't you worry yourself none about that,' stated the sheriff. 'I'll take a ride out to Fort Walsh once I've concluded my initial investigation.'

'You won't have to ride no place, the 'breed's still in town,' advised Ketchum. 'I saw him enter into the livery stable not five minutes ago.'

Bates sighed as Harry Stock, the town undertaker, arrived on the scene to take care of the body.

'OK,' he said, nodding at Ketchum, 'I'll go talk to him. Doc, can you and Harry take care of things here?'

Doc Stephens nodded. Bates then eased his way through the crowd and headed down the dust-bowl of Main Street, past the army ambulance which was waiting outside the hotel with its escort of four mounted troopers. The soldiers eyed him suspiciously as he passed by without a word or acknowledgement of any kind. The events of the previous summer had only served to add to the bad blood between the townsfolk and the military. As a result, the commanding officer at Fort Walsh, Major Turner, had declared the town off limits to soldiers for several months following the death of Sheriff Blaine. The ban had only recently been lifted, following lengthy discussions between the major and Bates. But suspicion and hostility still festered like a sore that would not go away.

In spite of the relatively early hour, it was already hot and humid, so the peace officer was sweating profusely by the time he reached the livery stable at the far end of town. He paused in front of the building, removed his hat, rubbed the back of his hand across his damp brow, checked that the pistol on his hip was loaded and then entered through the Judas gate in the main door to interrogate the notoriously quick-tempered Curly Smith.

The dusky-skinned scout was leading the palomino pony he had borrowed from a young friend at the fort, while his own mount was being reshoed, out of its stall at the rear of the building, when he came face to face with the unsmiling lawman. He halted directly in front of the sheriff, who stood rock-still, blocking his path.

8

'Can I help you?' he asked contemptuously, spitting out a chaw of black tobacco.

'Yeah,' responded Bates, unflinchingly. 'I want to take a gander inside your saddle-bags.'

'Why? What am I supposed to have done?'

'I got a dead man, minus his scalp and duds, lying in the alleyway between the saloon and the doc's place.'

'What's that got to do with me?' growled the half-breed.

'That's what I aim to find out,' stated Bates. 'As far as I know, scalpin' is a Comanche trait, and as you're the only Injun in town, I'm aiming to search you.'

'The hell you will!' exclaimed the scout, casually dropping his right hand to the butt of his Navy Colt. 'You ain't got no call to accuse me of killin' anyone. I've been here all night, seeing's how your fine townsfolk won't let me sleep in the hotel. I reckon you're just trying to cause more trouble with the army.'

Bates shook his head.

'That ain't so,' he insisted. 'I'm just trying to solve a murder, that's all. If'n ya have nothing to hide, you won't mind me looking inside your personables.'

'Get out of my way, lawman. I've a replacement officer and two new troopers to escort to the fort,' snarled the scout.

'You're not going anywhere until I've conducted my search,' insisted Bates.

'So you say!' roared the scout, his fingers closing

around the handle of his gun.

The sheriff's pistol cleared leather a split second quicker than his opponent's. At almost point-blank range he couldn't miss. His bullet caught the half-breed in the shoulder, sending him spinning away into the stall at his back as his gun clattered harmlessly on to the straw-covered floor. The scout's pony reared up in alarm at the sudden commotion, forcing the lawman to step aside in order to avoid being trampled underfoot. He deftly grabbed hold of the frightened animal's reins, quickly bringing it under control.

'That wasn't too smart of you,' he advised, holstering his gun as the Judas door banged open behind him.

'What happened?' demanded Ketchum, halting at his side.

'First Curly objected to my searching him, then he drew on me,' announced Bates. 'I reckon I'd like to see what he has to hide.'

'So would I,' said Ketchum.

'You ain't got no right to do this,' moaned Curly Smith through clenched teeth as he sat with his back resting up against the wall of an adjacent stall.

'We have every right,' corrected Bates. 'A man lies dead in the street, and your actions make you my number one suspect.'

'I didn't kill no one,' insisted the scout.

'What's going on here, Sheriff?' demanded an unfamiliar, gruff voice from the doorway of the livery stable. Bates and Ketchum half-turned to face the newcomer. There was something slightly incongruous about the man's military uniform and bearing, but Bates couldn't quite figure out what it was that struck him as odd.

'Who are you?' he demanded.

'Captain Randal Cummings, Fifth United States Cavalry. Now would you mind answering my question?'

'What's it got to do with you?' argued Ketchum.

The officer pointed to the wounded half-breed and said, 'It's got everything to do with me, friend. That man is an army scout, sent here to escort me and some new recruits to Fort Walsh. The troopers have just told me all about the vendetta you people have been waging against the military, but isn't this carrying things a bit too far?'

'Some would say we ain't carried it far enough!' retorted Ketchum.

'Easy, Hal,' said Bates, laying a firm but friendly hand on the carpenter's shoulder. He then nodded towards the scout. 'This ain't got anything to do with our dislike of the Yankee military, and besides, we don't rightly count scouts as being real army. But we do have reason to believe that Curly might have killed a man last night.'

'He's lying,' snapped the scout, wincing with pain, 'I've already told 'em, I didn't do it.'

'So, judging by the look of things, you shoot first and ask questions later,' observed the captain, a dead-pan expression on his deeply tanned face.

'Curly went for his gun,' replied Bates. 'I shot in self-defence.'

The captain snorted, then shook his head.

11

'I want this man turned over to me. If he's done wrong, he'll face an army court martial.'

'No way in hell!' roared Ketchum. 'Curly Smith's going to jail. He'll be tried right here in town, and then we'll hang him.'

'I can't allow that to happen,' said the captain, pointedly.

'I don't rightly see how you can stop us!' exclaimed Ketchum, defiantly.

'Counting the new recruits, I have six armed troopers waiting in the street outside,' replied the captain. 'I'd say I've got enough manpower to prevent a lynching.'

'There ain't gonna be no lynching, Captain Cummings,' stated Bates. 'I'm gonna search Curly's belongings, just like I planned to all along. If I don't find what I'm looking for, then you're free to take him with you, but if'n I find any evidence which ties him to the murder, then he stays here in the town jail 'til we can arrange for the circuit judge to hold a trial.'

The officer silently pondered the situation for a moment and then said, 'OK, Sheriff, we'll do things your way. Go right ahead and search this man's possessions, but I insist on remaining here to act as an impartial witness.'

Bates nodded in assent.

'This ain't right!' complained the scout, coming slowly and painfully to his feet as the sheriff moved his pony.

'I assure you this badge says it is,' replied Bates, removing the saddle-bags from the half-breed's mount.

He went down on one knee, unbuckling each bag in turn, emptying the contents on to the floor in front of him. A bloodied knot of black hair popped out of the second bag together with a small white canvas sack, tied up with a piece of thin string, which jingled loudly as it hit the deck. Bates picked up the scalp and threw it towards the half-breed scout.

'No wonder you didn't want me to look inside your saddle-bags,' he hissed, turning his attention towards the canvas sack.

'It ain't mine!' yelled Curly Smith, dropping it distastefully on to the ground. 'I ain't never seen it before. Someone must have put it there while I was sleeping.'

'Yeah, of course they did,' mocked a grinning Ketchum. 'I'd say we've just found our killer, Bob, wouldn't you?'

'Looks that way,' agreed Bates, scrutinizing the canvas sack he held in the palm of his hand. He tossed it a few inches into the air, then caught it again as it dropped. 'Coins, lots of 'em I'd say, judging by the weight and jingling in my hand. I suppose someone put the money in your saddle-bags too, eh?'

'No!' snapped the scout, clasping his wounded shoulder tightly. 'Give it back.' He took one step towards the lawman but then froze in his tracks when he saw the barrel of Hal Ketchum's rifle swinging up to cover him.

Bates untied the string around the neck of the sack, turned it upside down and emptied the contents into the palm of his left hand, whistling low as his eyes beheld the shiny gold coins.

'I didn't know the army paid its scouts so handsomely,' he said, glaring at Curly Smith. 'Could be I'm in the wrong line of work.'

'There ain't a mark on them,' observed Ketchum. 'I'd say they was all fresh-minted.'

'There's no way in hell you earned that scouting,' said Bates.

'He must've taken it from that stranger he bushwhacked in the alley,' declared Ketchum.

'How about it, Curly? Care to tell us how you came by the money?' demanded Bates, as he counted the coins back into the bag.

The scout glared at him but held his tongue. When the peace officer repeated the question, Curly Smith turned his head away from his accusers and mumbled, 'I ain't got nothin' to say to you.'

'You're going to jail, Curly,' said Bates. 'And you'll stand trial for murder.'

The captain didn't like it, and he said as much, but he had no choice but to leave the scout in the sheriff's custody. Having promised Curly Smith that he would speak with Major Turner, and arrange for legal representation upon reaching the fort, Cummings left the livery stable to rendezvous with his ambulance and escort.

'That there Yankee soldier-boy is a little too full of hisself for my liking,' observed Ketchum, spitting into the dust, as he and the sheriff led their prisoner towards the town jail. 'I reckon he's a riding for a fall.'

'He ain't no different to the rest of them there officers out at Fort Walsh,' advised Bates. 'But I tell you what, I reckon this is gonna stir things up again fer sure.'

II

Fort Walsh lay a long, dusty, bone jarring, four-hour ride from the settlement of Miller Springs. If anything, the army ambulance that the post's commanding officer had sent for Captain Cummings was even harder on his wiry frame than the Butterfield stage which had brought him most of the way west. He took a silent vow never to ride in any kind of a wagon again if he could possibly help it. At least astride a horse, like his escort and the two new recruits, a man could avoid most of the bumps and potholes that littered the trail. On the credit side, at least he had enjoyed some welcome respite from the burning sun, unlike his sweat-sodden, dust-covered escort.

It proved to be a trouble-free, if humid and boring ride through a flat, unchanging, parched and grassy landscape. When they rested briefly at a water hole midway between the fort and town, the captain broke with tradition and tried to engage the new recruits in conversation. There was seldom any social interaction between officers and other ranks.

They inevitably came from different backgrounds and had little in common, save for their loathing of Indians, the heat, the dust and the winged, biting insects that afflicted their daily lives. Despite his gentle probing, the men gave little away about themselves.

Jake Faraday, who seemed to spend the entire break scratching himself all over, claimed to be a farmer who'd hit upon hard times, due to a failed crop and an unsympathetic Yankee banker. He didn't seem to be the farming type, which made the captain feel that he was more likely to be a former Confederate soldier who had grown tired of trying to make an honest living since the end of the war and was now searching for a new battleground. The second recruit, Danny Jacobs, was little more than a boy. He volunteered no information about himself, other than his name, and as Cummings had no genuine interest in him or his former troubles, for all new recruits were invariably running away from something, he didn't press the matter.

By the time the single-storey, closely grouped, adobe-bricked buildings that comprised the lonely frontier outpost of Fort Walsh came into view, Cummings wanted nothing more than a cold beer to quench his thirst and a bath to clean the dust and soothe the aches from his battered body. The duty officer, Second Lieutenant John Ramsey, saluted the ambulance and escort as they entered the compound. Privates Vince Pritchard and Henry Rothwell, who were cleaning out the company stables, were promptly ordered to attend to the captain's needs. Pritchard hurled his pitchfork into a nearby bale of straw, wiped a forearm across his sweaty brow and then set off across the dry, rutted compound to where the ambulance had halted in a cloud of dust directly in front of the headquarters building. Rothwell delayed just long enough to complain under his breath about having to do something else which he hadn't signed on for before joining his more willing companion by the stationary, dust-covered vehicle.

'Pick up the captain's bag, Pritchard, and then take him to see the major,' instructed Lance-Corporal Seamus O'Flattery from his position atop the coach. 'You've got the team, Rothwell. Make sure you walk 'em for twenty minutes and then rub 'em down before feeding 'em some oats.'

'Dumb animals get better treatment than the troops around here,' muttered Rothwell as he slowly sidled up to the horses to do the corporal's bidding, casually side-stepping the newcomers who were descending on his side of the coach.

'That's 'cause they're smarter than you and work a darn sight harder!' stated the corporal, grinning from ear to ear. The private simply ignored him, for he suddenly had something else on his mind other than the dull, daily grind of army life. The arrival of the newcomers and a brief glimpse of a face had stirred a memory. Ever the opportunist, Rothwell was already figuring out how to turn it to his advantage. One thing was for sure, if he could work things out, he would be in a strong position to make capital of his knowledge.

When he heard the door to his private office open, Major Bart Turner looked up from the papers he was studying and smiled.

'Captain Cummings to see you, sir,' announced Sergeant Patrick Thomas, the duty NCO. Turner came to his feet and moved around his desk to greet his new second in command.

'Welcome to Fort Walsh, Captain Cummings,' he said. 'I trust your journey wasn't too tiring or unpleasant.'

'Unfortunately, it was both,' replied Cummings. 'I'm sore all over and feel like I could sleep for a week, but I'm here now and that's all that matters.'

Turner settled himself on the corner of his desk and gestured to Cummings to sit down in the chair directly in front of him. Once the captain had made himself comfortable, he wasted no time in telling the major about the trouble in town. He offered to return with a troop of cavalry to obtain Curly Smith's release, but Turner shook his head.

'We have to play things straight,' he said. 'This is a matter for the civilian authorities, not us. I know Bates, he's young and a mite headstrong at times, but he's nobody's fool. He'll ensure that Curly Smith gets a fair trial.'

'I hope you're right, Major,' said Cummings, drumming the fingers of his right hand on his knee, 'but with the mood in town this morning, I wouldn't be at all surprised if they end up lynching your scout.'

Turner frowned as he stroked his chin thoughtfully.

'In that case, I'll send Lieutenant Ratcliffe and a couple of troopers into Miller Springs, to make sure the townsfolk behave themselves until the circuit judge arrives.' He promptly called Sergeant Thomas into the room and instructed him to escort the captain to his quarters, see to his immediate needs and then find Lieutenant Ratcliffe.

Within the hour, Ratcliffe and a pair of veteran troopers were in the saddle bound for Miller Springs. Their orders were very explicit: report directly to Sheriff Bates, offer him full military co-operation in his investigation, evaluate the prevailing mood in town and take all necessary steps to ensure Curly Smith's safety until the trial. Ratcliffe had no liking for his assignment, mainly because he had no time for the truculent scout, having had several minor run-in's with him in the past, but he was not the sort of officer to question an order. At least, unlike the majority of the military personnel on the post, he did enjoy a reasonably good relationship with the young and scrupulously honest lawman, which was why the major had selected him for such a tricky assignment.

Turner was also well aware of the fact that the dashing lieutenant was known for his tact and diplomacy and an ability to remain cool under pressure. If anyone could avoid further trouble in what was potentially a powder-keg situation, it was the intelligent and popular Ratcliffe, whose men would have ridden through hell had he ever requested it of them.

The lieutenant wasn't the first person to leave the

post for Miller Springs that afternoon. When Miguel Diaz, the thirteen-year-old Mexican orphan who helped out around the sutler's store, heard about what had happened in town, he immediately decided to do something to help the scout. Curly Smith was one of the few people on the post to ever show him any kindness. Mexicans and Indians had always been regarded as second-class citizens by the vast majority of the troopers at Fort Walsh, and the prejudice they had been forced to endure had ultimately forged a sort of mutual bond of understanding between them, despite the difference in their ages.

Diaz didn't really believe that his friend was a murderer, but if he had indeed killed a stranger in town, then the youngster felt he must have had a good reason. Having packed his few possessions inside his bedroll, he stole the pistol his employer kept behind the counter in the store, and then set off for town on the storekeeper's Indian pony.

It was an uncomfortably sticky and oppressive night. As darkness fell the regular card-players amongst the troopers of C Company gathered around the small battered table in the centre of their barracks to pass the time until taps. Poker was the name of the game, and although the stakes were modest and losses corresponding small, everyone took it very seriously. It wasn't long before the moody Henry Rothwell was losing, as usual. He cursed loudly and threw in his hand as Vince Pritchard claimed a second pot in a row.

'You sure ain't no card-sharp!' observed the youthful Harry Jardine from his position at the unhappy private's shoulder.

'Shut your stinking mouth, kid!' exclaimed Rothwell, 'or you'll be losing something too – a few teeth!' The sniggering which immediately broke out around the table did little for Rothwell's disposition. He came tetchily to his feet, grabbing what little money he still possessed from off the table in front of him.

'Deal me out!' he snapped. 'I need some air.'

'How'ya ever gonna make good on your losses from the past three nights, if'n you quit the game now?' asked Owen York, the likeable veteran of the troop, with a sly grin.

'To hell with you, York!' sneered Rothwell, turning towards the door. 'To hell with all of yus! I don't need to worry about anything, not with the money I'm about to come into.'

'Some wealthy widow left you something in her will?' joked Jardine, to the merriment of everyone in the room.

'No, I reckon he's planning to rob the bank in town,' offered Pritchard, shuffling the deck as he prepared to deal another hand. Rothwell stood with his hand poised on the door-latch, shaking his head.

'You can laugh all you want,' he said, 'but a little knowledge can be worth more than any pot in your damn game. Jest wait and see, I'm about to become the wealthiest private in this man's army.' With that, he disappeared outside.

'What do you reckon he meant by that?' queried York.

'Hanged if I know,' replied Pritchard. 'Jest deal another hand.'

Rothwell quickly made his way across the moonlit compound towards the horse corral, totally oblivious to the splendid panorama of shimmering stars in the inky-blue skies overhead, intent on a quiet smoke and a period of reflection. Far out on the prairie a lone coyote howled at the rising moon. Rothwell smiled to himself as he considered how both he and the scavenger of the plains were hunting prey in their own way that night.

The trooper had always considered himself to be as good a poker-player as any man on the post, but the cards had sure been unkind to him of late. Now it appeared, at long last, that his luck was about to change for the better. He leaned back contentedly against the top rail of the corral and rolled himself a smoke, relishing the prospect of recouping his losses at the expense of a man who he was sure would want to keep certain details about himself secret from the officers on the post. It was often said that a little knowledge was a valuable commodity on the frontier, well he was about to put that time-honoured maxim to the test.

No sooner had the thought popped into his head than he heard a sound behind him. Before he could turn around the crook of an arm locked around his windpipe, cutting off his air-supply. He struggled for all he was worth but failed to break the choking hold on his neck. With a vicious, sudden jerk, his assailant broke his neck, letting him fall lifelessly to the ground. He was found, scalped and robbed of his pocket-book, an hour later by troopers from his own company, who had become concerned by his failure to return to the barracks by taps.

III

The two trail-weary riders paused atop the crest of the low hill, burnt yellow under the fierce glare of the Texan sun, and gazed down towards the sparkling waters of the shallow river fifty yards ahead of them. They were back in familiar territory, less than a day's ride from the Davis ranch, which was their immediate objective, after nearly three fruitless months in the saddle. It was also dangerous country, often frequented by roving bands of Comanche warriors, the fiercest tribe on the plains, and their cutthroat friends, the Comancheros, who plied their illicit gun and whiskey-running business from small isolated towns on both sides of the border. The country was vast, and post-Civil War Texas was still anything but civilized.

Only a matter of months earlier, the riders had been caught up in a bloody Indian raid. The memories of the horrors they had endured were still indelibly printed upon their minds. If he was to survive for long in such a hard and unforgiving land, a man had to be granite-tough and uncompromising and know the country and its ways like the back of his hand. Sam Kane, army scout, was just such a man, which was why his young charge, Daniel, had seldom, if ever, felt anxious or afraid in all the time they had spent together.

In spite of the inherent danger of travelling through the wilderness alone, it was true to say that with reasonable luck a man could ride for hundreds of miles without encountering any kind of trouble. Experience, an alert mind and a cool head were required, all of which Kane possessed in abundance. Now he was in the process of passing on his vast knowledge and well-honed survival skills to his young companion.

Kane knocked the trail dust from his clothes, then stood up in his stirrups to survey the lie of the land. Everything appeared quiet and peaceful. A quarter of a mile away, on the far bank of the river, he saw a family of deer approaching the gently rippling waters.

'Tell me what you see, Daniel?'

The boy instantly mimicked his mentor by standing up tall in the saddle to gaze all about him.

'The river's running low and slow,' he advised.

'What else?'

'The fact that the deer ain't in the least bit skittish tells me there ain't any large predators, neither man nor beast, on the prowl.'

Kane grunted in satisfaction.

'What about Indian sign?' he pressed. His young companion shook his head.

'Not a trace of Comanch' anywhere,' asserted the boy.

'You sure about that?'

The youngster pushed his hat back further on to his head and looked at him quizzically.

'Yeah.'

'What about those tracks at the water's edge?' queried Kane, pointing directly ahead of him towards a badly worn patch of ground. He kicked his mount into an easy canter, leading the way down the gentle incline towards the river.

Daniel was out of the saddle in a flash the moment they reined in. As his mount wandered leisurely forward to drink from the river, he went down on one knee to study the sign.

'Well?' asked Kane, standing at his shoulder. 'What do you make of it?'

'At least two wagons and several riders have crossed here in the past day or so,' the boy replied, standing up, beaming all over his face. 'All shod horses, not Indian ponies. I'd say it's an army supply train.'

Kane smiled and nodded approvingly.

'I'd say you're right. Though judging by the freshness of the dung those flies are buzzing around, I reckon the soldiers can't be more than a few hours ahead of us. They seem to be heading the same way as us, let's see if we can catch up with them.'

'Sounds good to me,' agreed Daniel. 'Especially if we can make it by supper-time; it'll make a pleasant change from having to suffer your cooking!'

Kane playfully kicked the youngster in the rump,

but immediately regretted it, for his bit of fun brought a sharp stab of pain to his right thigh. Although the wound he had suffered earlier that summer while fighting the Comanches had healed well, it had left a wicked scar and a slight stiffness as an unwelcome legacy of that almost fatal encounter.

'Let's ride,' he said, rubbing his leg before reaching for his horse's reins. 'We've got a lot of ground to cover if'n you want to dine with your soldier friends tonight.'

They experienced no difficulty in following the supply train's tracks as they travelled south-west through mile upon mile of dry, rolling, prairie grassland, under a burning-hot sun, ever watchful for any sign of danger. As well as the incessant heat, glare and high humidity, they also had to contend with a veritable plague of midges and flies. Such was life on the Texas plains in high summer, for while blood-sucking critters were plentiful, trees were few and far between and shade from the sun almost non-existent.

Around mid-afternoon they watered their horses at a small stream which slowly meandered its way leisurely across the parched plains. From the looks of the sign, the soldiers had briefly rested for lunch amongst a small grove of cottonwoods on the northern bank before proceeding on their way towards the distant frontier post of Fort Walsh. Kane advised Daniel that they were steadily closing the gap and would, in all probability, catch up with them by the time they made camp for the night. As it turned out, they met up with them a good deal sooner than expected.

Late in the afternoon Kane suddenly reined in.

'What is it?' queried Daniel, on seeing the scout shield his eyes from the glare of the sun as he stared towards the far horizon.

'Might be nothing, but then again it could be trouble,' replied his companion, pointing towards the barely visible flock of buzzards circling in the sky way up ahead.

The youngster's heart skipped a beat. He knew the presence of such scavengers of the air meant only one thing: something directly in front of them was either dead or dying. Kane withdrew the army-issue Winchester from his saddleboot, then gently nudged his mount forward at a trot. Daniel instantly eased his mount up alongside him. Until they were sure of what it was they were facing, they would proceed with caution and be prepared for the worst.

Half an hour later they rode up to what remained of the army supply train. Kane immediately told Daniel to stay back and look after the horses while he went in for a closer look. He didn't want the boy to see the grisly remains of the dead soldiers, who lay scattered where they had fallen.

The scout walked slowly about, studying the sign closely. One wagon lay broken and abandoned on its side in the tall grass, while the tracks of a second led due south. The six troopers had all been shot at close range, then stripped of their shirts, pants and boots. None had been scalped. This was not the work of any Comanche war party. Kane sighed and made his way back to where Daniel was standing patiently waiting with their nervous horses.

'Comanches?' asked the youngster, anxiously.

'No,' replied Kane, shaking his head. He squatted down, plucked a blade of grass from the ground and started to chew on it. 'Most likely Comancheros. I'd say the wagons must have been carrying something of value, either guns and powder or money to pay the wages of the soldiers at Fort Walsh.'

'Do you think they're still around?'

'No, they're long gone, boy. By now they'll be well on the way to the staked plains and a parley with their Comanche friends.'

'Are we going after them?'

'No we are not!' snorted the scout.

'So what are we gonna do?'

'Well,' replied Kane, discarding his chewed grass, 'I reckon we'll just head straight for the fort and tell Major Turner what's happened. It'll mean a delay of a day or so before I can get you out to Laurie and Debbie's place.'

'I don't mind,' Daniel assured him. 'I like it at the fort, you know that. Maybe Dick Squires will be there too.'

'Could be,' agreed Kane, hauling himself up into the saddle with a weary groan. 'That lazy no-good apology for a scout is never short of a reason for hanging around the fort when he should be working.'

'Ain't you gonna bury the soldiers?'

'What with? My bare hands? I ain't got no shovel and there sure ain't enough rocks around here to cover them up. The major'll send a wagon back for whatever's left of 'em.' With that, he led off at a trot towards Fort Walsh.

They rode into the open compound around mid-morning the following day. Having stabled their mounts, they made their way across the dusty parade ground, cordially acknowledging the greetings of many a familiar face, towards the headquarters building. When they stepped inside, the duty sergeant, the happy-go-lucky Irishman Seamus O'Mally, came around from behind his desk to shake hands with Kane and tousle a smiling Daniel's matted hair. He promptly ushered them in to see Major Turner.

'Kane, you're a sight for sore eyes,' said the commanding officer, rising up from his chair on catching sight of his visitors. 'I'd just about given you up for lost.' He extended his hand to the scout. 'I see you still have a saddle partner.'

'Yeah,' remarked Kane. 'Kinda had a problem getting rid of him. Things didn't exactly go according to plan.'

'So I heard,' replied the major. 'I'm sorry to hear about your aunt and uncle dying of cholera while you were *en route* to them, young Daniel, truly I am.'

'Thank you, sir,' said Daniel. 'But I reckon I'll be real happy if Laurie and Debbie will take me in, as Sam reckons they will.'

'There's no problem on that score,' insisted the major. 'They got your letter a few weeks ago, Sam. Laurie's already got a room ready for this little bub. Lieutenant Ratcliffe called at the ranch on one of his routine patrols last week. He said both Laurie and

Debbie are real excited about making Daniel part of their family again.'

'I figured they would be,' said Kane. 'At least I can get him out of my hair at last!'

'Hey!' exclaimed his young charge, slapping the scout on the arm with his hat. 'I thought you liked me.'

'I do,' Kane assured him with a grin, 'but that don't mean I want to adopt you! Now go get lost for a while, I need to discuss some business with the Major.'

'OK,' sighed Daniel. 'I'm gonna try and track Dick down.'

'He's definitely somewhere on the post,' advised the major. 'How about you and Sam having supper with my wife and me this evening?' The youngster looked expectantly at his friend, who promptly nodded.

'Sounds good to me,' said the scout. 'Now scoot.'

Once they were alone, Kane wasted no time in telling the major all about his grisly find out on the prairie. Turner shook his head and cursed under his breath. What he said in reply caused the scout to raise his eyebrows.

'It's the second army caravan they've hit this month,' revealed the major. 'Both were carrying a large consignment of Winchester rifles for the troops here and at Fort Concho. I'm damned if I know how they found out about the supply trains.'

'Once could be pure bad luck,' said Kane. 'Twice is a mighty big coincidence I reckon.'

'You think someone here at the fort is selling

information to the Comancheros?'

'Yeah, that's exactly what I think. Who knew about the supply trains?'

'Just about everyone on the post,' advised the major. 'It's nigh on impossible to keep such a thing secret for long, not that I'd even want to. It's good for morale to let these hard-pressed, short-handed troopers know they'll soon be issued with the sort of modern weaponry they need to fight the Comanche more effectively.'

'And now the Comanche will soon have their hands on them instead of your troopers.'

'That's not a pleasant thought,' offered the major.

'No it ain't,' agreed Kane, replacing his hat as he moved away towards the door. 'So I reckon we ought'a try to do something about it.'

'What do you have in mind?'

The scout paused by the door and turned back to face the major.

'Give me Ratcliffe and a dozen good men and I'll go get your guns back.'

Turner looked puzzled.

'You'll never find them. It'll be like looking for a needle in a haystack.'

'Maybe,' conceded Kane, 'but I'd like to play a hunch. What d'ya have to lose?'

'Nothing,' agreed the major. 'But you'll have to do without Ratcliffe. He's gone to Miller Springs to try and sort out some mess Curly Smith's gone and got himself into.'

Turner quickly explained what had happened in town. When Kane had heard him out, the scout expressed his surprise about the murder charge against Curly Smith. Although he had never got along particularly well with the half-breed, and was well aware of his quick temper, Kane had never figured him for a cold-blooded killer and said as much. He had to admit though, that the discovery of the gold coins and the scalp amongst his possessions certainly made him look guilty.

The major then told Kane about the trooper, who had been found scalped by the horse corral that morning.

'Things are getting a bit lively around here,' offered the scout. 'Quanah's bucks are certainly getting bolder. But back to business, who do I take in place of Ratcliffe?'

'My newly arrived second in command, Captain Cummings.'

'What's he like?'

'Hard to say,' replied the major. 'He's only been here for a day or so, but he seems pleasant enough, if a little stiff, and the men appear to like him. It'll be interesting to see how he handles himself in the field.'

'Which is why you want me along on his first official assignment away from the post.'

'Exactly,' confessed Turner with a rueful grin. 'You're a good judge of people, Sam. I look forward to hearing your opinion upon your return. Now, before you take your leave, I'd like to know just what you have in mind?'

'There's a small settlement on the banks of the Jerome River named Garston Crossing. I've heard tell it's a popular watering hole for Comanchero bands during the summer months. I aim to ride in to see what I can find out. I'll take Dick Squires with me. In the meantime, I'd have one of the other scouts try to track down that Comanche who snuck in last night. You need to find out if he's part of a raiding party.'

'OK,' said Turner. 'And good luck. Somehow I think you're going to need it, my friend.'

IV

Kane's plucky band of volunteers left the fort before dawn the next morning. As their line of march took them within striking distance of the Davis ranch, the scout had decided to drop Daniel off along the way. The youngster was excited about being reunited with his surrogate family, and as a result, he and his old pal Squires chatted and laughed incessantly throughout the long hot morning. Kane soon found their good-humoured conversation distracting, so he opted to ride up ahead on his own. Captain Cummings trotted forward to join him on his bay pony.

'First time in Texas, Captain?' asked Kane, as the officer drew alongside.

The captain nodded. 'How far is it to Garston Crossing?'

'About a three-day ride, as long as we don't encounter any trouble.'

'You seem to know the territory well, Kane,' observed the captain.

'I ought to,' replied the scout. 'I'm Texan, born and bred, and I've been scouting this country for the army for a parcel of years.'

'You didn't fight in the rebellion?'

'No, I guess I was in the minority in these here parts, for it 'twern't a cause I believed in. Slavery never did sit well with me, and though there were broader issues, such as Yankees imposing their will on the rest of us, it didn't bother me enough to go to war. I also had some pretty important personal business to attend to at the time, trying to track down the man who killed my mother.'

'I hear tell the Comanches made it tough on those who stayed behind,' said Cummings.

'Yeah, they did,' agreed Kane. 'The majority of the Texas Rangers enlisted in the Confederate army at the outbreak of the war, and the Yankees couldn't spare enough soldiers to fight Indians. It meant that the settlers on the frontier were left to largely fend for themselves. It's only now that we're truly beginning to claw back what we lost.'

'Are we likely to encounter any Indians on this patrol?' queried the captain.

'There's every chance,' replied Kane. 'This is Comanche country, but I sure hope to avoid them. We'll have our hands full recovering the rifles from their Comanchero friends without fighting off any roving war party too. Now, if'n you'll excuse me, Captain, I'm gonna ride on ahead a piece and check things out.' With that, the scout kicked his mount into a fast trot towards a line of low rolling hills a few miles ahead.

They reached the Davis ranch three hours after leaving the fort. The men watered their mounts and then enjoyed some of Laura's coffee and home-baked cookies under the shade of her porch while Kane and Squires helped to get Daniel settled. Little Debbie fussed over her new brother like an old mother hen, not that Daniel minded, for in truth he enjoyed all the attention. Kane was pleased to see how quickly the mental scars of the previous summer had faded away. The young are nothing if not resilient, he mused to himself as he settled back in the old rocking-chair on the porch to enjoy a second cup of coffee.

The same could have been said of the attractive widow who refilled his cup. Laurie had rebuilt both the ranch and her life since the Comanche raid which had claimed her husband. She had a herd of 500 head of longhorn cattle and a loyal, hard-working team of cowpokes to run the spread. Kane admired her for her courage and stubborn refusal to give up and move on to pastures new, which any other woman in her place would certainly have done. Had he been the ranching, settling down kind, he might even have made a play for her, but in truth, he liked his life, tough as it might be, just the way it was.

Within the hour, the patrol was back in the saddle and heading west towards the notorious settlement of Garston Crossing. Kane and Squires delayed just long enough to take it in turns to give their young friend and little Debbie a final hug. Promising to return when time allowed, they galloped hard to catch up with the captain and the troopers.

Despite the heat and the necessity to walk the horses every few hours in order to maintain their stamina, the patrol made good time. The men remained watchful and alert as they pressed on ever deeper into Comanche country. They were all too well aware of their enemy's ability to strike without warning from out of a seemingly empty land. Apart from the two new recruits, who had arrived at the post with the captain, all the troopers were well known to both Kane and Squires. They were good, experienced fighting men, who had ridden with the scouts on many a previous mission, and were therefore extremely unlikely to panic under pressure.

The expedition cut Indian sign twice during the afternoon, but had no direct contact with any hostiles. They did, however, encounter a company of Texas Rangers, out tracking a small war party who had raided a local ranch the day before. Kane and the Ranger captain exchanged intelligence and opinions, then wished each other good hunting as they headed off in opposite directions.

When the orange sun began to sink beyond the western horizon, the patrol made camp along the northern bank of a small, crystal-clear stream. No one voiced any objections when Kane insisted on cold rations. The troopers knew that lighting a fire to cook food or boil coffee would have been most unwise, for any Comanche buck worth his salt could detect smoke from miles away. Dried-beef jerky and cold beans wasn't exactly appetizing fare, but it kept their hunger at bay and greatly reduced the risk of detection.

Once he had eaten, Kane volunteered to stand the first watch. There was a restless tension hanging over the camp, which was to be expected given their situation. Squires relieved his friend at midnight when the silvery moon was high in the sky and the prairie deathly quiet, save for the peaceful chirping of the crickets down by the stream. In turn, he was replaced by the likeable veteran York, two hours later.

Kane had them back in the saddle at first light. They rode in single file through the tall, gently swaying grass, relishing the slightly cooling breeze that had sprung up from the south overnight, hoping their good luck would hold. Nobody spoke until the time came to dismount and walk their horses.

'What are you aiming to do when we reach the settlement?' asked Squires, reaching for his tobacco pouch.

'Leave you and the troopers a safe distance outside of town while I go in to see what I can find out,' replied Kane, reaching back for the canteen hanging from his saddlehorn. 'The sight of all those blue uniforms is likely to spook the *bandidos* we're after.'

'There ain't no way you're riding in there alone, friend,' insisted his companion, firmly, rolling himself a smoke. 'You're gonna need someone to watch your back, and I'm jest the man to do it.'

'OK,' agreed Kane happily, having taken a long swig of tepid water from his canteen. 'Just as long as you know what you might be getting yourself into. From what I hear tell, the good citizens of Garston Crossing ain't exactly your regular, honest, God fearing frontier folk. They're the scum of the earth who'd slit your throat as soon as look at ya.'

'Should be quite a party,' joked Squires, swinging himself back up into the saddle. 'I can hardly wait.'

Late in the afternoon of their third day on the trail, at the far end of a wide valley set between two gently sloping ranges of grassy hills, the column encountered a rutted trail, heading due west. Kane informed the captain that the well-worn road would lead them directly into Garston Crossing. Sure enough, just before sunset, the settlement came into view dead ahead of them. With Kane leading the way, the patrol immediately left the trail and rode on up into the hills a mile or so from town. In the rapidly fading light, he chanced upon a sheltered hollow which was out of eyeshot of the trail below. It was here that the scouts left the captain to set up camp for the night, while they rode on in to check out the Crossing.

'Does the place have any law?' queried Squires as they rode on towards the settlement beneath the clear, star-studded night sky.

'Yeah, but I doubt if it's honest,' advised Kane. 'We'll have a drink in the cantina and see what we can find out.'

The sound laughter, the gentle strumming of a Spanish guitar and a sweet female voice greeted their unobtrusive arrival in the adobe settlement. They tied their mounts to the hitching rail outside the noisy cantina in the centre of town and sauntered inside through the swinging doors.

An old, balding, rather rotund and sinister-looking Mexican was tending bar. In the far corner of the room an attractive, young, dark-haired, green-eyed *señorita* in a blue-gingham dress was singing a tender love-song to the accompaniment of a guitar, played by a shabbily dressed peon who was old enough to have been her father. Twenty or so equally unpleasant, suspicious-looking *hombres*, Mexicans, half-breeds and white frontier-trash, were in attendance, either standing at the bar or sitting at the tables, talking and drinking. Kane doubted if any of them had earned an honest day's pay in years, if ever. It was just the sort of place Comancheros always frequented. No one even appeared to notice the newcomers, save for the bartender.

'What'll it be, *señor*?' he asked, blandly.

'Whiskey,' replied Kane. 'And leave the bottle.' Kane wasn't truly a drinking man, but he felt it best to try to blend in with the rough company they were keeping.

'You're a stranger,' observed their host, blowing dust from the pair of glasses he set on the bar before them. He uncapped a bottle of cheap, rot-gut liquor and quickly filled each glass in turn.

'Here, but not other places,' replied Kane, non-committally.

'We tend to mind our own business in Garston Crossing,' said the bartender, with a dead-pan expression, 'but as we don't get too many visitors we are a mite suspicious of strangers. You two could be mistaken for Rangers.'

'No,' stated Kane, as he paid for the bottle, 'you have us pegged wrong, we sure ain't no lawmen. We're what you might call entrepreneurs. We buy and sell things.'

'Really?'

The scout nodded.

'And what exactly would you be in the market for?' asked the bartender, through narrowing eyes.

'Guns.'

'Then try the hardware store in the morning,' said their sneering host, turning away with the ghost of a smile to serve another customer at the far end of the bar.

Kane picked up his glass and the bottle and led the way across the dirt floor towards a corner table, which afforded them a good view of the hot, smoky room. It was not the sort of joint where a man would want to turn his back on anyone.

'What now?' whispered Squires, slowly casting his eyes about the room.

'Have a drink,' replied his companion with a grin as his eyes adjusted to the heady, smoky atmosphere within the busy cantina. 'But take it slow and easy and keep your wits about you. We need to sit tight for a while and see what happens.'

Kane's first sip of whiskey brought a slight grimace to his lips and a burning sensation to the back of his throat which almost caused him to gag. He knew that if they finished the bottle, they would be in no fit state to defend themselves if trouble flared. As the evening wore on, more of the rusty-coloured liquor surreptitiously found its way from their glasses to the dirt floor beneath their table rather than to their lips. To all intents and purposes, though, the bartender and anyone else taking a close interest in the newcomers would have felt sure they were much the worse for drink.

Throughout the evening they kept an ear cocked

for any potentially useful snippets of information. Kane had hoped that the bartender would drop the word to someone within the room that he was in the market for guns, but when midnight arrived and no one had approached their table, the scout gave it up as a bad job. He nudged Squires with his elbow and led the way slowly back out into the street.

'Let's take a ride down to the livery stable and see if we can find any trace of our wagonload of guns,' suggested Kane, keeping his voice low as he hauled himself up into the saddle.

'You really think they'd be dumb enough to bring it into town?'

'Probably not, but then again, you never can tell. The Comancheros probably consider this to be a safe haven. There ain't no real law to speak of, so I reckon they would feel they could pretty much come and go as they pleased.'

'Them rifles could already be in Comanche hands,' said Squires as he put his right foot in the stirrup. 'We might just be wasting our time.'

'Could be,' agreed his companion with a weary sigh, kicking his mount into motion down the street, 'but I'd be surprised if the trade's already taken place.'

They had ridden only a short distance when six men dressed in serapes and broad-brimmed sombreros suddenly materialized out of a dark alley-way to surround them. The scouts reined in to the click of Winchester rifles being brought to bear on them.

'Who are you?' growled a short stubby Mexican

standing directly in front of them. His manner and bearing made it plain that he was the leader. Given the odds facing them, Kane opted to talk rather than fight.

'I could ask you the same question!' exclaimed the scout, locking eyes with the *hombre* who stood rock-still in the street with a rifle trained on his chest. 'But then I already know the answer. You're Comancheros, probably the very *hombres* we've been looking for.'

'I told you zey were Rangers, Chico,' drawled a second Mexican from the sidewalk as two of his companions moved forward to disarm the scouts. 'I say we kill them now.'

Kane shook his head slowly.

'We ain't lawmen, and you'd be making a hell of a mistake if you kill us, friend.'

'What makes you say that, gringo?' queried the man called Chico.

'Because we're here on behalf of a man who has an interesting business proposition to put to you, so you'd be well advised to listen to what we have to say.'

'Keep talking,' advised their interrogator, his face expressionless, the rifle still rock-steady in his hands.

'We're here to buy guns for an ex-Confederate colonel, our former commanding officer during the War between the States, who's now living in exile in a hacienda below the border.'

'Why would such a man require guns?'

Kane smiled. 'You could say he's planning to renew hostilities with the Yankees.'

'What kind of guns is he looking for?' asked Chico.

'Repeating rifles,' said Kane. 'Like the one you've got pointed at me. As many as you can supply.'

Chico taking the hint, casually rested his Winchester over his shoulder, but his suspicious companions continued to keep the scouts covered.

'How much is your colonel willing to pay?'

'Top dollar, plus a bonus, for immediate delivery.'

The Comanchero had no liking for gringos, but didn't quite know what to make of the stranger who claimed to be a former rebel, out to refight the civil war. He knew he could just as easily be a Texas Ranger, out to bait a trap. However, Chico felt he was holding all the aces. If they turned out to be Rangers, he could kill them at his leisure, and if they were who they claimed to be, then he could take their money and still kill them! Then he would trade the rifles to Quanah Parker's Kwadies as planned, and double his profits. The twinkle in the Mexican's eyes betrayed his intentions.

'Of course, we're not carrying the money with us,' advised Kane, calm as you like. 'You can never be sure about what sort of bad company you might fall in with in a town like this.'

'So how were you planning to pay for ze guns then, gringo?'

'The money's with some friends of ours,' advised Kane. 'They're camped up in the hills, a short ways east of here. Once we've seen the guns and agreed a price, we'll take you to them.'

'Oh, no,' corrected Chico, wagging his finger to

46

and fro. 'First we see the colour of your money, then we trade. My men will go with you to your camp.' He turned and spoke rapidly in Spanish to the man at his side. His *compadre* grinned and nodded. 'Mano will bring you to our camp an hour after sunrise.'

'OK,' agreed Kane, 'but I warn you, friend, no tricks, my companions are all seasoned Reb troopers who know how to handle themselves when it comes to a fight.'

'You do not trust me, gringo?' asked Chico, feigning hurt.

'No!' stated Kane, locking eyes with the Mexican. 'I'm afraid I don't.'

The Comanchero laughed heartily, the sound echoing through the otherwise deserted street. 'I like you, gringo, I think we are going to get along just fine. There will be no tricks, as long as you have the money.'

'Oh, never fear, we have the money all right,' Kane assured him. 'And if things go smoothly in the morning, this could be the start of a long and mutually beneficial association.'

'Until tomorrow then,' said Chico as his men led the scouts away to where they had left their own horses. 'It should be an interesting day, no?'

'That it will be,' called Kane over his shoulder.

V

Squires rode at his friend's elbow, wondering what he had in mind. They had been unable to communicate in any way since leaving town, due to their escort of three heavily armed, highly suspicious Comancheros. It meant they were going to have to play things off the cuff and rely on their instincts and experience on reaching the camp. Most of the troopers were bound to be asleep. Success would depend upon the alertness of those standing guard. With luck the pickets would realize something was wrong when they heard so many horses approaching out of the darkness. It would then be a question of how quickly the other sleepy cavalrymen reacted to the danger in their midst.

The moon was already on the wane by the time Kane reined in, fifty yards from camp. He turned to face the Comancheros and said:

'I need to let my friends know it's me or they're likely to shoot first and ask questions later.'

'Go ahead,' said Mano, 'but just remember, I'll

have a gun trained on your back, just in case you're thinking of pulling any tricks.'

'I wouldn't dream of it,' replied Kane. 'We need those guns of yours.'

'Just take us in slow and easy,' hissed the Mexican, cocking the hammer of the Navy Colt he held menacingly in his right hand. Kane nodded, swung back to face the trail ahead and discreetly winked at Squires, as he kicked his mount into motion up the slight gradient.

'Hello the camp, it's Kane, we're coming in, and we have some company.'

'Come ahead, Sam,' cried a voice the scout instantly recognized as trooper York's. 'It's always a pleasure to welcome guests.'

Kane gambled that the private's statement meant he had heard the riders approaching and had already alerted his sleeping comrades. He made his move the moment they crossed the picket line. Before the Comanchero at his back could react, the scout rolled off his mount, slipped between its legs and sprang up like a cat to knock the *bandido* off his mount. At the same time, Squires leapt towards a nearby sagebrush, clearing the field of fire for the soldiers hidden in the darkness.

Kane and Mano rolled over and over in the dirt, desperately grappling for possession of the outlaw's pistol, as hot lead filled the night air. In the mêlée the Mexican managed to land a vicious punch to the side of his jaw. Kane's head snapped back violently, but he managed to raise a hand to ward off a second blow while maintaining a tight grip upon his opponent's gun hand. Stunned but fighting mad, he forced the Comanchero over on to his back, pinning him to the ground. He tore the gun from the bandit's hand and brought the barrel crashing down on his exposed skull. Mano grunted loudly, then lay still.

While Kane and his opponent were locked in personal combat the soldiers kept the other two Comancheros fully occupied. The troopers held the advantage, for they were able to shelter behind the small bushes and rocks scattered about their camp-site. They were also able to locate their targets by listening for the sound of their horses milling about in the confusion and by the occasional flashes from the desperadoes guns.

By the time Kane came to his feet, all the opposi-tion had been accounted for. Squires came to meet him as he recovered their hardware from Mano's saddle. Kane handed him his pistol and Winchester as the captain came forward to join them.

'Is he dead?' asked Cummings, pointing towards the prostrate figure at the scout's feet. 'I hope not!' exclaimed Kane, holstering his own Navy Colt. He casually slipped his Winchester back into its rightful place in his saddle boot. 'Assuming you killed the others, he's the only one who can lead us to the miss-ing guns.'

The scout quickly brought the captain up to date on what had happened in town and all they had learned. It was then that Pritchard called out that one of their number was down. 'It's Yorkie. He must have stopped a bullet during the fight,' he said as the rest of the patrol formed up around the dead soldier, who lay face down on the ground. Blood seeped from a wound in the middle of his back.

'God damn!' exclaimed Squires. 'York was one of the best men I ever served with. Him and me have seen some action these past few years, I can tell you. We've helped each other out of many a tight fix.'

'He was the best friend I ever had,' sighed Pat Halliday, as Pritchard respectfully draped a blanket over his fallen comrade. Halliday and the dead veteran, together with young Johnny Gannon, had been almost inseparable. The trio were excellent soldiers, almost invariably amongst the first to volunteer for any dangerous assignment. Their fearless reputation and knowledge of the Comanche had guaranteed them places on the current mission the moment they stepped forward to offer their services. They had all been with Kane the previous summer when he had ridden after a band of renegade troopers who had killed the sheriff of Miller Springs when drink had got the better of them on a visit to the town.

'Do you think our prisoner will talk?' hissed the captain, nodding towards the unconscious Mexican.

'Oh, yeah,' promised Kane, who had been deep in thought, dimly aware that something was bothering him, 'he'll talk all right.' He turned to face Dick Squires. 'Stake our friend out good and tight, then throw some water over him. I'll be right back.'

'Where are you going?' queried Squires.

'To find me an ace in the hole,' replied Kane,

having collected a small canvas sack from his saddle-bags.

'I have a horrible feeling I know what you have in mind.' Kane merely grinned. 'You really are one mean son-of-a-bitch!'

'Yeah, and I'm proud of it.'

He disappeared into the night, returning a short while later with a bulging sack which rattled menacingly. It confirmed Squires's worst fears. Without a word, Kane moved swiftly towards the spot where Mano lay bound to four wooden pegs, driven firmly into the ground. He stood over him and gave the sack a little shake. The chilling sound brought a look of pure terror to the Comanchero's bloodied face as he tried desperately to tear himself loose of his bonds, but all he succeeded in doing was rubbing his wrists and ankles raw.

'Where will we find your pal Chico and the guns he stole from the army?' growled Kane.

'Go to hell!' sneered Mano, renewing his painful and fruitless attempts to break free.

'Wrong answer,' advised Squires, as Kane began to untie the cord he had secured around the neck of the sack.

'You can't let him do this!' wailed the Mexican, pitifully.

'I don't rightly see how we can stop him!' stated Squires, spitting out a chaw of tobacco. 'Now of course, if you were to tell us what we wanted to know, then Sam here might be more inclined to listen to reason.'

'Chico will kill me if I talk!'

'And this here rattler will kill ya if you don't,' said

Kane, turning the bag upside down. When the large, angry diamondback landed on the ground, it immediately coiled up in the striking position, inches from the terrified Comanchero's bare feet.

'OK, OK!' he screamed. 'I'll tell you, I'll tell you, I swear it.'

Kane swiftly and effortlessly kicked the snake away into the brush.

'Chico will be waiting for us in a box canyon, about five miles due north of town,' said Mano. 'That's where we stashed the rifles.'

'When were you planning to trade them to the Comanches?'

'Quanah's due to meet us around noon tomorrow.'

'And who's your contact at Fort Walsh?' demanded Kane forcefully, nudging him in the ribs with the toe of his boot.

'I don't know what you're talking about,' replied the Comanchero, staring up at the scout through hate-filled eyes.

'Sure you do,' insisted Kane. 'I want the name of the person who's been selling information about army supply trains, or maybe I need to fetch me another rattler?'

'No!' yelled Mano. 'Someone at the fort is helping us, but I don't know his name.'

'How does this fella manage to get word to Chico when a shipment of rifles is due?'

The Comanchero told him what he wanted to know. Kane listened patiently while the renegade explained how easily the information was passed on.

What he said made perfect sense. Whenever a consignment of arms and ammunition was expected, the traitor sent a cryptic message, written in Spanish, to Chico via the general store at Garston Crossing. There was never any shortage of Chicanos or apparently tame Indians hanging around the post, and they were always willing to carry a letter for a few dollars and the promise of a bottle of whiskey at journey's end.

'And how does Chico pay his informant?' asked Kane.

'In gold. They met up sometime last week in the town of Jasper. That's all I know.'

Kane felt sure his captive was telling the truth. Come morning, he planned to recapture the guns and take the renegade leader alive. Then he would be able to fit the final piece to the puzzle and hand the traitor over on a plate to a grateful Major Turner.

The two scouts settled themselves down on the edge of camp, within sight of their prisoner, safe in the knowledge that Pat Halliday, an Irish trooper whom Kane knew particularly well, and Vince Pritchard, were standing watch until first light. Squires was just dozing off when he heard Kane suddenly jump to his feet.

'Trouble?' he asked, looking all about.

'No,' replied Kane, 'but I do need to go check on something.'

When Squires saw his friend walk over to where the body of Owen York lay covered by a saddle blanket, he got up with a sigh and wandered over to join him. By the time he arrived, an intrigued Halliday and Pritchard were also in attendance.

'Did anyone see York fall?' asked Kane, keeping his voice low in order to avoid disturbing the slumbering cavalrymen.

'Yeah,' said Halliday. 'I did.' He described how he had seen York collapse to the ground while loosing off a shot in the heat of battle. The scout massaged his stubbly chin thoughtfully.

'Is it likely he could have got in some other trooper's line of fire where he was standing?'

'No,' insisted Halliday. 'We were spread out pretty good, thanks to your timely warning. That was smart thinking, Kane.'

'Where is all this leading?' asked Squires. Kane took a deep breath.

'York was shot in the back,' he said, 'which means he was murdered in cold blood by a member of this patrol.'

'You can't be serious?' gasped Halliday. But Kane insisted that he was deadly serious. 'Why would anyone want to kill ol' Yorkee? I don't reckon he had an enemy in the world.'

'Well, it sure looks like he had at least one,' interjected Pritchard, 'and we have to root the bastard out and string him up.'

'That might be easier said than done,' said Kane. 'Whoever it is, he's one devious son-of-a-bitch, and he's hardly likely to do anything to give himself away.'

'So what do you suggest we do then, Kane?' demanded Halliday.

'We'll keep this under our hats, for now, and watch each other's backs until we make it back to the fort,' replied the scout. 'Then we'll tell the major what we know and let him decide what he wants to do about it.'

'I reckon we have some interesting days and long nights ahead of us before we can rest easy again,' observed Halliday. 'There's no telling if he has some-one else on his shit list.'

'I'd say you're right,' agreed Kane. 'Now if'n you gents will excuse me, I aim to catch a couple of hours sleep while I can.'

VI

The patrol was in the saddle before the sun appeared above the eastern horizon. With Kane, Squires and the sullen Mano riding point, and Halliday and Pritchard warily bringing up the rear, the column skirted around the hills where they had spent the night, before cantering north-west towards the box canyon and their rendezvous with the Comancheros.

Kane had interrogated their captive to ascertain how best to approach the camp. He and Cummings had then agreed upon a strategy which called for the scouts, the prisoner and two troopers disguised in the clothing taken from the dead Mexicans to ride in alone. The rest of the patrol would scale the canyon walls to get the drop on the bandits when Kane arrived to collect the shipment of rifles.

As the spectacular pink and red hues of predawn gave way to the pure azure of a typical Texan summer's morning, their guide brought them to a halt in front of a range of rocky hills which contrasted sharply with the scorched plains they had been traversing. Mano sat back in the saddle, raised his tightly bound hands, then pointed directly ahead.

'That's where they will be waiting.'

Kane nodded as he drew his knife and cut through his prisoner's bonds.

'No tricks,' he warned, 'or the first bullet will have your name on it.'

The column arrived at the canter with Cummings at its head. He reined in beside Kane and said, 'Are you sure you can trust this Mexican?'

'I don't trust him one little bit,' replied the scout. 'But our friend here knows the score. His first mistake will be his last.' The captain nodded.

'Good luck,' he said. 'We'll support you when the shooting starts.'

The sound of approaching horses and a warning shout from the man standing guard by the entrance to the canyon brought Chico and his band of a dozen cutthroats to their feet. Coffee cups and breakfast plates were hurriedly cast aside as they reached for their rifles and fanned out in front of the stolen army supply wagon to face the approaching riders. When he recognized his friend Mano and the gringo who wanted to buy guns, the bandit chief relaxed, letting his hands fall away from the pistols on his hip. Mano's other two companions had reined in close to the mouth of the canyon and were deep in conversation with the guard.

'Welcome, *amigo*,' cried Chico, spreading his hands wide apart in greeting. 'Have you brought gold to pay for the guns?' Kane shook his head. 'Silver?'

'Just lead.'

'Oh, no, no, no, *señor*,' said Chico, smiling and wagging his finger from side to side. 'You cannot buy anything with lead, except death.'

'That's right,' agreed the scout without a flicker of emotion. 'And right now there are around a dozen guns trained on you and your *compadres*, so if you're of a mind to, you can buy all the graves you like.'

'You are joking, no, *amigo?*'

Kane shook his head solemnly as he watched the Mexican slowly lower his hands towards his gunbelt.

'Touch those guns and you're a dead man.'

'Who are you?'

When Kane told him, the Comanchero spat contemptuously on the ground.

'Oh, well,' he snarled, 'I guess I'll just have to kill you!'

He went for his guns, but before they cleared leather, a bullet from the scout's Navy Colt caught him right between the eyes, sending him sprawling backwards into the coffee-pot simmering over the fire. A second bullet accounted for the Comanchero who was in the process of drawing a bead on him with the Winchester he had instantly shouldered when trouble flared.

Mano instinctively threw himself at Kane, knocking the gun from his hand as they fell to the ground. All about them gunfire exploded from the rocks high above the floor of the canyon as the Comancheros dived for cover behind the stolen wagon and their saddles. Mano and Kane rolled over and over in the dirt, trying to gain the upper hand, each with an arm around the other's neck. The scout grunted loudly when the Comanchero managed to land a solid blow to his ribs. Despite the pain in his side, he managed to wrestle his way clear of the tight grip upon his neck. He landed a roundhouse right of his own which caught the outlaw flush on the jaw. Two more telling blows to the head effectively ended the fight, freeing Kane to join in the gunfight still raging all about him.

As he came to his feet a bullet pinged into the dry, sandy earth exactly where he had been lying. When he looked up, he caught sight of a Comanchero skulking behind the wagon with a rifle pointed at him. The scout rolled athletically over in the dirt and came up firing from the hip. Although all three of his shots failed to find their mark, they forced the outlaw to duck back out of sight behind the wagon as wooden splinters filled the air. It provided Kane with the time he needed to reach the cover of a boulder a short distance away.

It was all over within minutes. One by one the *bandidos* fell under the merciless, unrelenting gunfire from above. When Kane realized the Comanchero guns had fallen silent, he emerged from his hidy-hole waving his arms high in the air, calling for the troopers to cease fire. All the Comancheros were dead, save for Mano, who remained out cold.

By the time the other troopers joined them in the canyon, Mano was trussed up and the crates of stolen rifles had been found in the back of the wagon. They had got what they came for and in so doing had also permanently cut one of Quanah Parker's main supply lines. Kane emerged from the wagon just as Cummings cantered into the encampment.

'Good work,' he said, dismounting smoothly. 'Did you find the guns?'

Kane swatted a bothersome fly, then pointed back over his shoulder in the direction of the wagon.

'Yeah, they're still in their shipping crates. Now all we have to do is make it back to the fort in one piece.'

'You think we're likely to run into further trouble?'

'We're many a long mile from Fort Walsh, and deep in Comanche country, Captain,' replied Kane. 'Quanah's bound to come after us when he finds out what's happened here.'

'But we can make it?' asked Cummings, as Dick Squires joined them.

'Sure we can, with a bit of luck,' interjected Squires, 'but we have to keep our wits about us. Out here the first to make a mistake is generally the first to die.'

'What about them?' The captain gestured towards the dead Comancheros.

'Leave them where they fell,' advised Kane. 'Every minute counts. Throw Mano into the wagon and have the men water their mounts. I want to be on the move in ten minutes.'

'So be it,' agreed the captain, moving away to address the troopers.

'We did good,' observed Dick Squires.

'Yeah, we did,' agreed Kane, 'but I came mighty close to taking a bullet in the back of the head, and it wasn't from any Comanchero rifle either.'

Squires frowned.

'If'n I'd been a split second later in moving after taking care of our friend Mano, I wouldn't be standing here talking to you. And the puff of dust it sent up meant it could only have come from behind me.'

'Well, if'n you're right, pard, then it looks like our killer has decided to make you his next target,' observed Squires, as they collected their mounts. 'Mind you, it could be worse.'

'How do you figure that?' queried Kane.

'Well, he could have chosen me!'

VII

The unforgiving sun beat down remorselessly from out of a cloudless sky upon the heads of the patrol as they rode steadily eastwards, in a high state of alert. They maintained as fast a pace as they dared, given the need to conserve the energy of their mounts and the distance they still had to cover, but by noon, when they stopped to eat and rest a spell, the patrol was still perilously close to the staked plains the Comanche claimed as their own. Although the heat, energy-sapping humidity, dust and ever-present annoying myriad of biting insects were their only visible concerns, Kane was convinced Quanah would come after them.

As if that wasn't enough to worry about, the scout knew he also had to watch his back for the enemy within. The shot which had narrowly missed him back in the canyon only served to confirm that the murderer of trooper York also wanted him dead, though he had no idea why. He continuously racked his brains, trying to think of a reason why any of the troopers would want to kill him but, try as he might, he drew a blank.

Kane had always enjoyed a healthy relationship, based on mutual respect, with all the soldiers at Fort Walsh, save for the arrogant, vicious, rebellious sergeant Hobbs, who had eventually turned renegade a year earlier. When the sergeant had gunned down Sheriff Bates's predecessor during a visit to Miller Springs, the scout had chased him and his murderous companions half-way across the territory before bringing them to book.

As the day wore on, the oppressive conditions took their toll on the column as they journeyed on in an almost zombie-like trance across the seemingly endless grassy plains. During the heat of the afternoon several troopers dozed in the saddle, only to be jolted awake a split second before toppling to the ground. Only Kane and Squires seemed able to maintain their high level of concentration throughout the day.

Late in the afternoon, the landscape began to change. Once they had forded Little Squaw River, pausing just long enough to water their mounts and enjoy a brief respite from the glare of the sun amongst the thick grove of cottonwoods growing along the banks, the flat plains gradually gave way to broken country littered with dry ravines and rolling hills. The scouts became even more wary, for it was perfect ambush country.

The sun had almost slipped below the western horizon when Kane decided to make camp for the night alongside a tiny, almost dried-up stream which provided just enough water to meet their immediate needs. Squires completed a wide loop around their bivouac to ensure there were no hostiles in the vicinity. Upon his return, Kane gave permission for the troopers to light a small fire to enable them to enjoy some hot coffee with their cold rations.

'I swear I've forgotten what hot food tastes like!' exclaimed Halliday, strolling over to join the scouts on the edge of the camp, where they were listening intently for any unusual sounds emanating from the darkened prairie.

'Me, I'm gonna have myself the biggest steak I can lay hands on, once we're back at the fort,' stated Squires.

'You figure we're gonna make it?' asked the trooper, gazing out into the gathering darkness.

Kane shrugged his shoulders. 'Hard to say. It mostly depends on when Quanah found his Comanchero pals. Provided we've got a big enough head start, we should make out OK.'

'I'm just as worried about the asshole within this patrol who's using us for target practice,' advised Pritchard, keeping his voice low, as he came over to join them. 'There's no tellin' who might be next.'

'I reckon I know,' interjected Kane. It was his first opportunity to bring them up to date with what had taken place during the gunfight back in the canyon. His account did little for Pritchard's peace of mind. Nor did the sudden, spine-tingling, mournful howl from somewhere on the far side of the stream. 'It's just a coyote,' advised Kane on seeing the nervous troopers instantly reach for their sidearms.

'I've been thinking,' said Pritchard, letting his hand fall away from the pistol on his hip. 'Maybe York wasn't the killer's first victim.'

'What makes you say that?' queried Kane, with a frown.

'Well, this afternoon I remembered something Rothwell said on the night he died. We was all ragging on him for losing at cards again, then he went off outside bragging about how it didn't matter one little bit, seeing's how he was about to come into a lot of money, due to him knowing something important. A short while later, we found him minus his scalp.'

'I don't see what you're drivin' at,' said Squires, tilting his hat back on his head. 'Rothwell jest got plumb careless and ended up getting his hair lifted by some Comanche buck.'

'I reckon there could be more to it than that,' insisted Pritchard. 'Rothwell was always out to make a fast buck. The way he spoke sort of gave me the idea he might be indulging in a bit of blackmail.'

'And you've no idea who his target was or what he knew?' asked Kane.

Pritchard shook his head. 'No, he was always one for playing his cards close to his chest. But I reckon we can say for sure that whatever he knew, it got him killed.'

'Maybe he found out who's selling information to

the Comancheros,' suggested Halliday.

'That would certainly provide a motive for his murder,' agreed Kane. 'But it doesn't explain where York and I tie in to all this. There must be a reason why we're on the killer's death list, but I'm damned if I can figure it out.'

'So what are you aiming to do?' pressed Halliday.

'What I said before, stay alert, rely on you fellas to watch my back and wait for whoever it is to make a mistake,' replied the scout. 'It's all I can do.'

'I know every man jack of this patrol almost as well as I know myself,' said Halliday, 'save the two new troopers, Faraday and Jacobs. I've fought beside them, drunk with them and played cards with them more times than I can remember. I'd trust each and every last one of them with my life, so, if you want my opinion, our killer has to be one of the newcomers.'

'Yeah,' agreed Pritchard. 'The killings didn't start until they arrived at the fort.'

'That's as maybe,' said Kane, 'but how do you explain the fact that the Comancheros were hitting our supply trains long before the new troopers rode in. If there is a link between the raids and the murders, it would seem to rule them out.'

Before Pritchard could argue the point, another long, mournful coyote call echoed from afar, causing Kane to turn away from the conversation to scan the dark prairie. Squires instantly moved to his friend's side. Kane's almost imperceptible nod sent Squires on his way to warn the captain that danger threatened.

'What is it?' asked Halliday.

'That was no lonesome coyote. We have some unwanted company,' replied Kane, keeping his voice low as he moved towards the spot where the horses were picketed. 'It looks like we're set for a little night riding.'

The mere mention of the word Comanche was sufficient to galvanize the sleepy troopers into action. Tired as they were from four days on the trail, they were in the saddle within minutes. With Kane at the head of the column, Squires riding drag and the wagon carrying the guns and the prisoner in the middle, they headed due east at a canter beneath the bright yellow moon, with only the clinking of bridles, sabres and canteens to be heard. It was imperative they found a suitable defensive position by sun-up, for if the Comanches caught them out in the open, they would be swiftly overrun.

The eerie moonlight illuminated the rugged terrain, making it comparatively easy for Kane to keep the column moving at a brisk trot. It also meant that if the hostiles chose to attack, the soldiers would be able to see them coming. Kane was banking on his experience and knowhow to keep them out of trouble.

Hour upon weary hour they rode on beneath a starry canopy. Nervous eyes constantly scanned the ghostly, hostile landscape for any sign of the ruthless enemy who was stubbornly and relentlessly dogging their trail. Quanah Parker was not going to let the repeating rifles slip through his grasp without one devil of a fight. With the moon finally beginning to wane and the first trace of grey, predawn light registered in the eastern sky, the patrol reached Weeping Woman Creek. They quickly watered their mounts, before fording the shallow creek and resuming their desperate flight.

By sun-up the anxious, dust-caked patrol was still more than half a day's ride from the safety of Fort Walsh. Both men and horses were on the point of exhaustion, while the Comanches remained hot on their tail. Cummings urged his mount forward at the canter to consult with Kane, keen to know what the scout had in mind.

'We can't outrun them, can we?'

Kane shook his head. 'No we can't,' he conceded. 'We have to find a likely spot to make our stand.'

'Isn't there an old abandoned Spanish mission not too far from here?'

'Yeah,' replied Kane. 'The Mission of Don Miguel. It's a crumbling ruin, but shelter of a kind. I guess it's a good a place as any, if we can make it.'

He immediately changed course, leading the column south-east towards the old adobe church, which had been abandoned for some thirty years or more. As he remembered it, the mission was located in a broad treeless plain, close to a stream, a landscape which would afford the hostiles precious little cover if they launched an attack. Although their food supplies were largely depleted, there was a good chance they could ward off the Comanches for several days and make them pay a heavy price for any bold frontal assault. However, given the nature of the prize on offer, it was highly unlikely that Quanah would give up easily.

The patrol was less than a mile from their objective when a series of high-pitched war cries filled the air. Dick Squires swung about, cursing under his breath at the sight of twenty brightly painted warriors rapidly bearing down on the rear of the column. Off to the left, a similar number were racing through the tall grass, hoping to cut the soldiers off from the comparative safety of the crumbling walls. Kane read their intentions. He instantly kicked his mount into a flat-out, lung-bursting gallop towards the mission, bellowing at the soldiers to do likewise.

Gunfire and shrill war whoops echoed across the land. Two bullets slammed into the wagon inches from the panic-stricken driver, throwing wooden splinters high into the air. An arrow thudded into the boards at the private's feet as he fought to control the team. Squires appeared at his side to offer much needed encouragement.

'Keep going!' he screamed above the noise of the wheels thundering over the bone-hard ground and the chilling, excited yells of the Comanches, who were gaining on them all the time. 'We're gonna make it!'

None of the troopers bothered returning fire as they forced every last ounce of energy from their flagging mounts. The walls of the mission were drawing tantalizlingly closer with every stride, but so were the savages to the rear. It was going to be a desperately close-run thing.

Just when it seemed the Indians would overhaul the wagon and its escort, gunfire exploded from inside the mission. A slug caught the leading Comanche buck flush in the chest, tumbling him from his pony. He was trampled underfoot as the rest of the war party maintained their pursuit. Two more shots rang out from the mission in quick succession, each finding its mark. The surprised warriors instantly broke off their attack, wheeling away from the ruined church, firing from beneath their ponies' necks.

The troopers swept into the dusty compound through the crumbling archway which had once supported a pair of stout wooden gates. They swiftly dismounted, drew their carbines and dashed to the low walls to repel the raiders who were regrouping out on the grassy plain. Kane grabbed hold of Squires by the sleeve of his buckskin jacket, pointing his carbine in the direction of the wagon.

'Break open those new repeating rifles,' he said. 'They might just give us an edge.'

Without waiting for a reply, he dashed towards the walls to join the soldiers, but as he did so, a familiar face suddenly materialized in front of him.

'Hello, Kane,' said Curly Smith, resting his Winchester across his shoulder. 'I certainly didn't expect to run into you way out here.'

'Nor me you!' exclaimed the scout, with a deadpan expression. 'I assume it was you who fired on the Comanches while we were heading in?'

Curly Smith nodded.

71

'Ain't you fighting on the wrong side?'

'I ain't no renegade, Kane,' he insisted, locking eyes with his fellow scout.

'That ain't what other folks say.'

'I don't care about that, I ain't done nothin' wrong, apart from busting out of jail, and I only did that to avoid being lynched.'

'How'd you get away?' asked Kane.

'My little orphan friend Miguel sneaked out from the fort and slipped me a gun through the bars of the cell window,' he replied. 'I used it to persuade the deputy to release me before I clubbed him over the head and locked him in the cell. Then I sent the kid back to the fort and hightailed it out of there.'

Kane grunted loudly. 'And I suppose you're gonna tell me you didn't kill the *hombre* they found in the alleyway in town?'

Curly Smith sighed and shook his head.

'You know me, Kane,' he said, defiantly. 'I'll admit I've done a lot of things in my life that I'm not rightly proud of, but I sure ain't no cold-blooded killer.'

'All the evidence says otherwise,' corrected Kane, standing his ground. 'A person might also suspect that you've been selling information about weapons shipments to the Comancheros.'

'Who ever says such is a lying son of a bitch!' roared Curly Smith.

'Ah reckon you need to postpone your private little parley,' advised Squires, halting alongside them, arms laden with brand-new repeating rifles. He nodded towards the prairie beyond the walls. 'Looks like them Comanch' are about ready to pay us a visit.'

Before Kane could reply, the air was filled with spine-tingling war whoops as the Indians charged the beleaguered defenders sheltering behind the less than secure walls of the mission.

VIII

The attack was over almost before it had begun. A dozen mounted braves, riding like the wind, firing from beneath their ponies' necks, charged towards the walls, then veered away when they came within rifle range. It was a Comanche tactic Kane was all too familiar with, having experienced it many times before. They were testing the defenders' firepower, playing on their nerves, keeping them guessing, trying to wear them down. Quanah had no need to launch a full-scale attack and risk the lives of his battle-hardened warriors. He could afford to wait it out, hit them with lightning raids and try to panic them into making a fatal error of judgement.

The warrior chief also knew a protracted siege would work in his favour. The soldiers could not escape. If they tried to make a run for it, even given the advantage of their better weaponry, the Comanches would soon cut them down. However, if they stayed holed up behind the mission walls, they would eventually run out of food and water. Quanah held all the aces, and he knew it.

Kane knew it too, but for the time being he was happy to sit tight and see what happened. There was little chance of aid, for no one knew where they were or that they were in danger. It would be many days before the major would consider them missing and dispatch a search party. There was always a chance of a Ranger patrol cutting the war party's trail and following them to the ruined mission, but it was a long shot. In essence, the soldiers could count on no one but themselves to get them out of their tight fix.

Throughout the long, hot hours of daylight, the Indians grew ever bolder, riding ever closer to the walls of the mission to draw fire, before galloping away to safety. The soldiers expended much valuable ammunition in warding them off, but suffered just two minor flesh wounds during the numerous sporadic attacks. For their part, the Comanches lost only two horses, and in both cases the riders were swiftly picked up unscathed by their skilled and daring companions. This only added to the growing sense of frustration and fatigue amongst the soldiers, whose lack of sleep was affecting both their aim and their nerves.

Early on in the siege, Kane arranged for whatever food and water they possessed to be strictly rationed. He also suggested to Cummings that the troopers should take it in turns to man the walls, allowing others to catch up on their sleep. Although this idea found favour with the captain, few of the soldiers managed to get any proper rest between the raids due to a combination of fear and the intense, sweltering heat.

Each fresh attack affected the already fragile morale of the men skulking inside the dusty compound. The chances of relief were slim and sooner or later their provisions would run out. There was also the small matter of the Comanches willingness to attack under the cover of darkness. Once night fell, there would be nothing to prevent the Indians from sneaking right up to the walls. They outnumbered the besieged troopers by at least three to one, which meant that if they managed to breach the walls, the defenders' fate would be quickly sealed.

'What are you thinking, pard?' queried Squires, handing his tired-looking friend some dried-beef jerky as he gazed out at the deceptively quiet, empty, sun-burnt prairie. The sun had just vanished behind the hills, darkness was less than an hour away, and a million mosquitoes were on the prowl, trying to beat the Comanches to the soldiers' blood. Kane irritably squashed one of the evil-looking, highly persistent, buzzing insects against his bristly, exposed face.

'I'm thinking I'd rather be somewhere else!' he observed with a wry grin.

'You and me both,' replied Squires, swatting at his own winged attacker. 'You reckon they'll move when darkness falls?'

His companion nodded.

'Yeah, though the moon should be bright enough to make them a mite wary.'

'With our luck, it'll probably be a cloudy night!'

quipped Squires, as they were joined by a worried-looking Captain Cummings.

'I assume they'll attack come nightfall?' he said, declining Squires's offer of a piece of unappetising jerky with a shake of his head. Kane merely nodded as he chewed on his dried meat. 'What are our chances?'

'I'd be lying if I said they were good,' advised Kane, 'but if the moon stays big and bright, we should be able to see them coming, and that'll help our cause some.'

'Enough to make a difference?'

'We'd all better hope so, Captain, or our top-knots will be dangling from Comanche war lances before morning, and I'm kinda partial to mine!'

'You've fought them often enough, what advice would you offer me?' asked Cummings.

'Make sure all the men are in position before the light goes,' interjected Squires. 'Them new Winchesters we handed out are likely to see a lot of service tonight.'

'There is another course of action open to us,' announced Kane, as a daring possibility took root in his scheming mind. The captain frowned. 'We could always try the unexpected.'

'What do you mean?' queried Cummings.

'If the situation was reversed,' said Kane, pausing to swallow another chaw of the tough beef jerky, 'what's the last thing you would expect your enemy to do?'

'Attack,' replied the captain, 'but you can't seriously suggest we leave the compound and fight in the open against a superior force?'

'That's exactly what I am proposing,' corrected Kane.

'But it would be plain suicide!'

The scout shook his head.

'No,' he insisted, 'the more I think about it, the more sense it makes. We can't simply wait out a protracted siege. Even if they don't manage to over-run us in the dark, it's only a matter of time before our food and water runs out. They are bound to wear us down in the end. I'll admit, what I'm proposing is risky in the extreme, but it could work. If we can kill enough of them during a surprise attack, Quanah might just figure the price is too high to get his hands on the guns.'

'You think he'd just give up?'

'Yeah,' said Kane. 'Quanah's nobody's fool. He's a popular and skilled war chief, but he knows he can't afford to lose too many warriors in battle. The Comanches follow him because they trust him to bring them great honour and splendid victories, but his reputation is also based on keeping his fighting men safe. If we make things truly hot for him, his bucks will undoubtedly put pressure on him to head home.'

'But they'll know we're coming,' argued the captain, 'and if they catch us out in the open, we'll be slaughtered.'

'That ain't part of my plan!' said Kane. 'The trick is to do the unexpected, to effectively use the element of surprise to turn the tables. In order to do that, we need to act quickly and quietly, before they realize what's happening.'

He quickly outlined his plan. When the captain had heard him out, he fired a series of questions at Kane, all of which the scout answered to his satisfaction. Cummings finally gave his consent, at which point Kane issued some instructions to Squires before setting off to talk to the troopers. He needed six battle-hardened, experienced men to carry out his audacious plan. In spite of the inherent danger facing the would-be raiders, Kane soon found his volunteers. It came as no surprise to him that Pritchard and Halliday were the first to step forward.

'Count me in,' said Curly Smith, approaching Kane and his party.

'No,' replied Kane firmly, shaking his head. 'You're staying put.'

'You don't trust me? You think I'll take off in the dark?'

'It ain't that,' stated Kane, trying to sound friendly. 'But with me and ol' Dick outside the walls with these here soldier-boys, I'm gonna need someone on the inside who can handle things if the wolf gets amongst the chickens. The captain's new to this country, he ain't fought Indians before, you have, which is why I'm leaving you behind. But jest make sure that when we come hightailing it back in, you hold your fire until you're certain it's a Comanch' you've got in your sights!'

'You're taking a chance, Kane,' said Curly. 'If'n I am a renegade, I could shoot you down like a rabid dog in all the confusion, and no one would know it was me.'

'That's true,' conceded the scout, 'so it jest goes to show how much faith I have in you, don't it, Curly?' The half-breed smiled. 'Now, before I take my leave of y'all, there's something I have been meaning to ask you, my friend, about the night you got yourself into trouble in town.'

Kane led him away towards the far side of the compound where they could not be overheard. Once they were out of earshot of the troopers, he asked the half-breed a number of probing questions about his visit to town and how he had managed to escape from jail. When he had finished his impromptu interrogation, Kane sent him on his way, satisfied that his fellow scout had spoken true. He felt he was now much closer to knowing the identity of the traitor who was supplying information about the weapon shipments to the Comancheros, but he still could not figure out how it tied in with the deaths of the soldiers and the attempt upon his own life. However, he felt sure that time, patience and careful observation would eventually help him to solve the puzzle, as long as the Comanches didn't get him first!

Timing was everything. If the volunteers moved too soon in the gathering dusk, the Comanches would inevitably spot them and the element of surprise would be lost. However, if they delayed too long, there was every chance the Comanches would attack first and Kane's desperate plan would go up in smoke. He therefore had his force slip over the walls the very moment full dark settled upon the still, windless, arid plains.

Keeping low to the ground the troopers quickly

and stealthily made their way towards the river. They did not exchange a single word as they quickly filled the water canteens they had brought with them from the compound. Having successfully accomplished their secondary mission, they silently fanned out in a wide arc along the western bank of the river. With faces blackened by the soot from the fires that had boiled their coffee, they lay on their bellies, virtually invisible to the naked eye, ready for action. Each man carried two, fully-loaded Winchester repeating rifles and a sidearm. All they could do now was lay still, keep their wits about them and listen for the pounding of horses' hoofs which would herald the arrival of the Comanche raiders.

They didn't have long to wait. Within minutes of settling themselves upon the rock-hard, parched earth they felt the tell-tale vibration of many riders cantering towards them. Then came the constant drumming of approaching war ponies, faint at first, but growing louder by the second. Fingers automatically and nervously tightened around the triggers of eight Winchester rifles. Any moment now. Each man knew exactly what he had to do. Kane's orders had been very explicit: on his command, all guns would open up on the enemy and keep on firing until empty, at which point they would hightail it back to the compound in the ensuing confusion, on foot if they had to, on captured Indian ponies if they got lucky.

The scout held his breath as the unsuspecting Comanches bore down on them from out of the darkness. When he heard the leading ponies hit the water he nimbly jumped to his feet and roared, 'Let them have it!'

All around him, gun flashes lit up the darkness. The leading warriors were cut down in mid-stream before they even realized they were under attack. In the pandemonium that ensued, several startled war ponies reared up, unseating their riders as they tried to turn them about in order to escape from the withering wall of fire emanating from across the river. One unlucky warrior managed to dodge a bullet that almost parted his hair, only to be trampled underfoot by his prancing mount.

Although the soldiers couldn't see the enemy, the terrified whinnying of the Indian ponies coupled with the panic-stricken yells of the confused warriors told them where to aim. Bullet after bullet unerringly found its mark, turning the silvery water black with blood under the rising moon. The Indians were too concerned with trying to save their own hides to bother returning fire. Their only thought was to flee into the night. Some made it, many didn't.

'Let's get out of here!' yelled Kane, on realizing that they had the prairie to themselves. The relieved soldiers didn't need any second bidding. They took off towards the mission without so much as a backward glance.

The ambush was over in minutes. The troopers had no way of knowing how many casualties they had inflicted upon the war party, and in truth they didn't really care. All that mattered was that they had boldly carried the attack to the enemy and had successfully routed them without suffering so much as a scratch.

'Hold your fire,' cried Kane as they approached the walls of the ruined church. 'We're coming in.'

'I assume your mission was successful?' said Captain Cummings as Kane strolled across the dusty compound towards him.

'I'd say so,' replied Kane with a deadpan face. 'Hard to say how many of them we killed, but we sure caught them by surprise and gave them something to think about, and we didn't lose any of our own in doing it.'

'You think we're in the clear now?'

Kane shrugged his broad, tired shoulders.

'Ain't no way of knowing for sure,' he said. 'But I doubt if they'll be of a mind to attack again tonight. If nothin' else, we've bought ourselves some more time.'

The captain nodded. 'So what do we do now?' he queried, happy to bow to Kane's experience and knowledge of fighting Indians.

'Well,' replied Kane, 'I don't know about you, but I aim to catch me some shut-eye.' And with that the scout wandered away to find himself a comfortable spot for the night.

IX

Kane was awake as dawn broke. He rose stiffly from the ground to stretch tight muscles and aching limbs, prior to folding up his bedroll. All around him weary troopers remained sound asleep, some snoring, some so still and silent they could have been mistaken for dead men, save for their rhythmic breathing. To a man they had earned this peaceful respite from the rigours of their dangerous venture. There was still every chance they would see action again soon, so whatever rest they managed to snatch was OK by him. The fresher the man, the clearer his head, and the better he fought when the chips were down.

A familiar face materialized at his side, as if by magic, to thrust a much needed cup of coffee into his hand.

'Thanks,' he said, nodding gratefully.

'Seems mighty peaceful out there,' stated Squires. 'You reckon we drove 'em off?'

'Could be,' offered his companion, savouring his

first sip of the sweet, steaming-hot coffee. 'We'll know for sure soon enough.'

Once they had drunk their coffee, the scouts roused the slumbering troopers. The weary men ate cold rations washed down with the hot coffee Squires had brewed for them, before taking up station behind the walls. The atmosphere remained tense, the men watchful, as the sun rose into the bright, clear morning sky. Within an hour it was so hot and sticky the men were sweating at their posts, but everything remained perfectly tranquil beyond the crumbling walls.

'What do you think?' asked Cummings, joining the scouts by the archway.

'I'm thinking it's time I went out for a look-see,' replied Kane, using the sleeve of his buckskin jacket to wipe away a bead of sweat trickling down his brow.

'Is that wise?' queried the officer, frowning. 'They might still be hiding close by, just waiting for us to ride out.'

'That's why I'm going alone,' insisted the scout. 'All being well, I'll be back within the hour and we can be on our way home.'

'And if you're not?'

The scout smiled. 'Then at least you'll know for sure they're still out there.' He turned to face Squires. 'You and Curly keep an eye on things until I return.'

'Sure thing,' agreed his friend. 'Watch your top-knot!'

Kane headed straight for the river. He paused briefly to study the sign from the ambush of the night before. The grass on the far bank showed traces of dried blood, confirming that many a bullet had found its mark in the dark. The Indians' line of retreat led due west. Kane eased his mount forward at the canter across the flat, treeless plain. It seemed empty and peaceful enough, but appearances could be, and often were, deceptive in such wild country, which was why he remained alert.

He soon came across the spot where the raiding party had made camp while besieging the mission. The bones of a pair of large deer, the remnants of their evening meal, lay scattered about the ashes of their cooking-fires. He found further traces of blood in the trampled grass round about. The ambush had clearly been successful. Heavy casualties had been inflicted upon the savages. He could tell from the tracks leading away from the camp that the Comanches had left in a hurry.

Kane returned to his mount and set off after them, intent on making certain they were heading home with their tails between their legs. He followed their sign for several miles before turning back towards the mission, satisfied that Quanah had given up on his quest to recover the guns. The patrol could safely resume their return journey to Fort Walsh.

As Kane rode into the compound he immediately sensed something was wrong. Squires came to meet him as he dismounted.

'Curly's gone,' he said, patting the neck of his friend's mount.

'What do you mean, Curly's gone?' demanded Kane. 'Didn't you try to stop him?'

'Couldn't,' insisted Squires, 'no one saw the going of him. He must have taken off some time during the night.'

'Well how come neither of us heard him?' queried Kane. 'Seeing's how we're both such light sleepers and all?'

His fellow scout shrugged his shoulders and spat on the ground.

'I don't know,' he sighed, 'but I'll tell you something even stranger, he left on foot.'

'Now that don't make a lick of sense!' exclaimed Kane. 'Curly's many things, but he sure ain't stupid, and only a stupid man, or a greenhorn, would set hisself afoot in this country.'

'Well, he's good and gone,' insisted Squires.

'Something's not right here,' said Kane, shaking his head. 'Have you looked to see which way he was headed?'

'No,' replied Squires, 'I figured to wait for you.'

'Well I'm back, so let's get to it.'

The scouts were half-way to the wall when Captain Cummings strode across the compound to intercept them. His dusty tunic was unbuttoned, he had yet to shave and his eyes suggested a distinct lack of sleep. He looked like a man carrying the troubles of the world upon his shoulders as he rubbed at his chaffed neck.

'I assume Squires has told you Curly Smith is missing?'

Kane took his hat off, twirled it in his fingers and nodded.

'What about the Comanches?'

'Gone,' replied Kane. 'I reckon we're in the clear, so we'll set off for the fort just as soon as Dick and me run Curly to ground.'

The scouts sidestepped the captain and began to circumnavigate the outside of the ruins, searching for any sign of the half-breed's passing. Both men prided themselves on their ability to find and read sign as well as any Indian tracker, yet they both drew a blank. It was as if their quarry had literally grown wings and flown the coop.

'What do you reckon?' asked Squires, removing his battered hat to scratch his matted hair as they stood outside the entrance to the compound pondering the situation.

'I'm thinking that our friend never left the mission,' replied Kane.

'Well, there sure ain't nowhere he could be hiding inside the compound,' argued Squires.

'There must be,' insisted his companion. 'Let's check it out.'

They quickly set about investigating every last nook and cranny of the ruined mission. Kane was determined to leave no stone unturned in their search for the missing half-breed, whose saddle and bedroll remained propped up against one of the crumbling walls of the church, where he had settled himself down for the night. Having covered just about every square inch of the compound, they were about to admit defeat when a casual comment from Private Gimenez provided them with a new lead to follow. The Mexican, intrigued by their conduct, had strolled over to join them in front of the church.

'What are you gentlemen looking for?' he enquired with a frown.

'Any place within the compound where a man could hide,' replied Squires, irritably. 'But I'm damned if we can find one.'

'Perhaps you're not looking in the right place,' offered the Mexican, grinning slyly. 'Try the well.'

'What well?' queried Kane. 'There ain't no well here. The brothers used to fetch their water from the river.'

'Sure they did,' agreed Gimenez. 'Once the well ran dry.'

'So where is it? We ain't found hide nor hair of one during our search.'

'Follow me,' said Gimenez, beckoning them with a flexing finger.

The Mexican led them along the side of the crumbling walls of the church to the back of the dusty compound. He stopped a few feet from the rear boundary wall and pointed down at the ground right in front of him.

'A few inches beneath the dirt you'll find some wooden boards,' he advised. 'They were put there to cover the shaft when the well ran dry. I'd be careful though, they've probably rotted through by now.'

'The sand has been disturbed quite recently,' observed Kane, moving past the trooper to commence digging in the earth with his bare hands. 'I have a nasty feeling about what we're likely to find.'

Kane quickly scooped the sand away to reveal half a dozen rotting boards covering an area about three foot by three foot. Once the boards had been pulled away, they found themselves staring down into an ancient, dried-up, adobe-bricked well, at the bottom of which lay the body of Curly Smith, lying sprawled grotesquely on his side with his neck broken.

'Fetch the captain,' ordered Kane, as Gimenez gave a low whistle and crossed himself.

'You think our killer's struck again?' queried Squires, when the scouts were alone.

'Sure looks that way,' sighed his companion. 'The way I figure it, our murderer must have been afeared Curly knew something which might give him away.'

'Well he sure ain't gonna tell us anything now,' said Squires.

'You'd be surprised what tales dead men can tell if you know how to ask the right questions,' replied Kane.

'You ain't talkin' any sense, pard,' insisted Squires with a puzzled grin. 'Ah reckon you've been out in the sun a mite too long!'

'Not at all,' argued his friend, good naturedly.

'What you aiming to do, hold a seance?'

'No need, finding Curly like this has already told us plenty.'

He was about to elaborate when the captain arrived at the run with Gimenez in stride beside him. Cummings eased past the scouts without a word to peer over the edge of the well.

'I guess he must have fallen and broken his neck while trying to hide out,' he said.

'Curly was murdered, Captain,' replied Kane.

'And just how did you come to that conclusion?'

'Easy,' interjected Squires. 'He could hardly have

replaced the sand over the boards to cover his tracks once he'd fallen into the well.'

'He was probably dead before he went into the well,' advised Kane. 'I'd hazard a guess that someone snuck up behind him last night and broke his neck before dumping him down there.'

'Who would want to do such a thing, especially at a time when the patrol might still be in danger?' demanded the captain.

'Probably the same person who murdered trooper York, and then tried to kill me,' stated Kane very matter-of-factly.

'What are you talking about?' roared Cummings, incredulously. 'York was killed by those Comancheros you brought back to camp.'

Kane shook his head. 'No he wasn't. Yorkee was deliberately shot in the back by a member of this patrol, undoubtedly the same varmint who took a pot shot at me during the gunfire with the Comancheros in the canyon.'

'Kane's called it right,' said Squires. 'There is a black-hearted killer amongst us.'

'So what do you suggest we do?' asked the captain.

'First we should bury Curly,' said Kane. 'Then we'll head for home with all the speed we can muster. The place for further reasoned debate is back at the fort.'

'Agreed,' stated Cummings. 'We'll leave within the hour.' He turned to face Gimenez. 'Arrange a burial detail, Private.' The Mexican nodded, saluted and took his leave at the double to do the captain's bidding.

'When we set off, I'll take the point and Dick can

ride drag,' said Kane. 'That way we can keep an eye out for trouble at both ends of the column.'

'OK,' agreed Cummmings. 'But who's going to keep an eye on both of you?'

'What do you mean?' demanded Squires, belligerently.

'Well if there really is a killer skulking amongst us, how do I know it's not one of you two?' queried the captain with a deadpan expression. He turned away to rejoin his men.

'You know what, pard?' said Squires, rubbing his chin thoughtfully. 'I really don't like that fella!'

X

A deep sense of unease pervaded the hearts and minds of every member of the troop as they made their way back to Fort Walsh, suffering in silence beneath the unrelenting glare and debilitating heat of the unforgiving sun. Whether the tension was a result of the spine-tingling memories of the recent deadly encounter with the savage Comanche raiders, and the fear that battle might be renewed before they reached the safety of the isolated frontier outpost they called home, or of the worrying rumour, started by Private Gimenez and spreading through the ranks, that an assassin was hiding in their midst, was hard to judge. Suffice to say that no one would relax until the fort came in sight.

Kane kept the column moving eastwards at as fast a pace as he deemed prudent. He was convinced the Comanches had given up the chase, which meant that with any luck the patrol would reach their objective some time during the afternoon, their mission successfully accomplished. However, the dark shadow of death hanging over them prevented him from feeling any sense of elation.

From where he rode, fifty yards ahead of the column, ever watchful, Kane's finely tuned senses never relaxed for a moment. The troubled scout reviewed everything he knew about the killings which had taken place and how they might be linked to the Comanchero gun-running operation. Clearly, someone had something to hide. The murders were not merely random events, the work of some psychotic malcontent who killed for sheer pleasure. There was a reason for each of the deaths, but one which completely eluded him. What did the victims have in common? What secret did they share? Why had they been sent to meet their maker? The more he debated the matter back and forth within the confines of his mind, the less sense he could make of it. The killer could not be the same person who had sold information about the arms shipments to the Comancheros, for Kane was fairly certain he already knew his identity, and he was back at the fort. So was he dealing with two totally independent desperadoes, or were they linked in some way? He shook his head. There was simply no way of knowing, at least not until he got to talk with the person he suspected of being in league with the gun-runners.

When the sun was at its zenith, Kane called a brief, welcome halt as the patrol approached a shallow, pebbly stream about a four-hour ride from the fort. The dust-covered troopers dismounted stiffly to water their horses before relaxing beneath the shady canopy of the tall cottonwoods growing along the western bank. Some ate cold rations, others stretched out on the ground to ease aching muscles and weary limbs, while the rest sat silently contemplating their lot.

Squires sidled up to where Kane stood with his back against the broad trunk of a cottonwood, hat pulled down over his eyes, deep in thought. Kane nodded towards him as he sat down on the bare, sunbaked earth, chewing on a piece of hardtack. They didn't exchange a single word until Squires had finished his unappetizing meal.

'Can you make any sense of it all, Sam?'

His companion shook his head, then pulled his hat up from over his inscrutable eyes.

'No, I can't,' he confessed. 'But at least we achieved our main objective. We recovered the guns and also put an end to one of the Comanches' main suppliers.'

'Yes, siree,' agreed Squires, 'we did that all right. Though I reckon if'n we don't find out who their contact was at the fort, our traitor will soon find hisself another renegade outfit to do business with.'

'Ain't no doubt about it,' offered Kane. 'Which is why we have some nosing around to do once we make it back to the fort.'

Once they were back in the saddle, with Kane leading the way, the scout's thoughts soon returned to the matter of the unsolved crimes. Counting the unidentified stranger in town, the first victim, four men were dead. Were all the killings the work of one and the same man? It didn't seem likely. The odd one out was clearly the poor unfortunate in Miller Springs, who in all probability had simply been the hapless victim of an opportunist crime.

Kane had no doubt that Curly Smith was not the guilty party. What the half-breed had told him back at the mission, before someone broke his neck, had convinced him his fellow scout had been conveniently set up to take the fall. However, he was equally certain the other three murders, those of troopers Rothwell and York, plus Curly Smith, had been committed by the same person, for the men all shared something in common: a military background. Furthermore, each of them had been based at Fort Walsh. Whatever the motive for the killing spree, whether it was related to the gun running, or some other unsavoury business, he was unsure, but one thing he did know, the common denominator was the Fifth United States Cavalry, and he was not going to rest for a moment until he got to the bottom of things.

A couple of hours from the fort, Kane had the troopers dismount and walk their horses for half an hour. Their long ride had left their mounts feeling the pace as much as the bone-weary soldiers, who themselves were sorely in need of some proper rest and hot food. Dick Squires eased himself up alongside Johnny Gannon, the youngest recruit on the post, and one of the most popular. His boyish, handsome looks and sense of fun belied a deadly skill with knife and gun, coupled with an ability to stand toe to toe with any man in the outfit when the going got tough. He had already fought the Comanche on numerous occasions during his fourteen months in the army and had won the respect of even the oldest, most demanding veterans. Just like York and Halliday, the youngster had fought right alongside Kane when the scout had ridden out after the renegade Sergeant Hobbs.

'I won't be sorry to see the fort,' he confessed, grinning at Squires as he reached for the canteen hanging from his saddle horn. 'I reckon I could sleep for a week.'

'Fat chance in this man's army!' exclaimed the scout. 'They'll have us back out on some other, godforsaken venture before we have chance to spit, you mark my words, boy.'

'I reckon you're right,' agreed Gannon, taking a long swallow of water from his canteen. He immediately grimaced at the unexpectedly acrid taste in his mouth as the tepid liquid slipped uncomfortably down his throat. 'Even the goddamned water tastes of dust out here,' he complained, hanging his canteen back over his saddle-horn as they strode on side by side across the rock hard, dusty ground.

The young cavalryman had taken no more than a dozen steps when he suddenly stopped dead in his tracks, clutching his stomach, gasping for air. Shock and pain were etched on his sunburnt face as he sank to his knees, coughing violently. He quickly keeled over on to the ground, where he lay writhing in agony as Squires and the nearest troopers rushed to his aid.

'What is it? What's wrong?' demanded Squires.

Gannon looked up at him through terrified eyes, which seemed to say, please help me, as his entire

97

body convulsed violently every which way. His legs thrashed wildly about, then, suddenly, he ceased struggling, his head falling limply to one side.

'What the hell's going on?' demanded Captain Cummings as he arrived on the scene, just ahead of Kane.

'Gannon's dead,' said Squires, removing his hat and shaking his head sadly. 'It looks as if he's been poisoned.'

'Bring me his water canteen,' said Kane, going down on his haunches beside the dead cavalryman for a closer look at his pallid lips. 'I reckon it'll tell us what we need to know.'

'I'll get it,' offered Pritchard, stepping towards Gannon's mount. He removed it from the saddle horn and tossed it to Kane. The scout removed the cap and took a whiff of the contents. When that failed to tell him anything, he took a small sip of the water, which he swilled around his mouth and then quickly spat out.

'The water's bad,' he said. 'Gannon's been poisoned all right.'

'But how could they do that without being seen?' queried Pritchard.

'It wouldn't be too difficult,' insisted Kane, standing up to hand the canteen back to the trooper. 'Our killer most likely made his move while everyone else was relaxing.'

'That ain't no way for any man to cash in his chips,' sighed Pritchard.

'Just what the hell's going on here, Kane?' queried a very concerned-looking Jake Simmons, a particularly close friend of the deceased. 'Who would want to do such a thing?'

'I don't have a clue,' confessed Kane. 'But what I do know is there's a cold-blooded murderer in our midst. He's now killed three times.'

'Three times!' exclaimed Pete Flanagan, one of the more experienced members of the patrol. 'What are you talking about, Kane?'

'First he killed York, then. . . .'

'Hold on there just a cotton-picking minute!' interrupted Simmons. 'Yorkee was killed by the Comancheros.'

'No, he wasn't,' said Kane, tipping his hat further back on his head. He then told them all he knew about what had happened since they had left the fort.

'Are you serious?' demanded Flanagan.

Kane nodded. 'Deadly serious.'

'But why would anyone want to kill York, Smith and Gannon?'

'I don't know,' replied Kane. 'But I sure aim to find out.'

'So what do we do now?' asked Captain Cummings.

'Throw Gannon over his saddle and head for the fort,' said Kane. 'We'll let the major decide how he wants to handle things.'

'All right,' agreed the captain. 'Let's get moving.'

XI

Upon the patrol's return to Fort Walsh, Kane and Squires reported directly to Major Turner. Captain Cummings was left to supervise the stabling of the mounts, the confining to barracks of the unhappy, utterly exhausted troopers and the transfer of their Comanchero prisoner to the guardhouse. The soldiers themselves would not be allowed any personal liberty until an official investigation into the murders had been completed, for the major would not run the risk of the guilty party absconding before he could be brought to justice.

By the time the captain reached Turner's office, Kane had already completed his report. While the major was understandably euphoric about the recovery of the guns and the wiping out of a band of cutthroat Comancheros, he was perplexed by the murders. They debated the matter back and forth while cutting the dust from their throats with some of the major's whiskey.

Kane refused to speculate either about possible suspects or motives when Turner tried to press him for answers. He would not even commit himself on the issue of whether the killer was linked in any way to the traitor selling information to the Comancheros. Only when he was alone with the major, Cummings and Squires having taken their leave to find some much needed chow and sleep, did he confide his suspicions as to the identity of the renegade living on the post.

'Are you sure about this, Sam?' asked Turner, pouring his trusted scout another slug of whiskey. 'It seems a mite unlikely, given his age and all.'

'I know it does,' conceded Kane, pausing to sip some of his whiskey. 'But the circumstantial evidence sure as hell makes the kid look guilty as sin.'

'Run it all by me again,' instructed Turner, toying with his half-empty glass.

Kane quickly recapped the facts as he saw them. The young Mexican orphan, Miguel Diaz, often left the post on errands for Fernando Juárez. His casual employment gave him a place to sleep, food to eat and the freedom to come and go very much as he pleased. No one would even notice if he went missing for a few days. By listening outside closed doors and open windows and generally keeping his eyes and ears open around the fort, he could easily gather the sort of information any unscrupulous renegade would give his eye-teeth for. He had both the time and the opportunity to conduct his clandestine activities without ever arousing suspicion. And if he did get caught listening at doors, who would ever suspect his true purpose? After all, he was merely a poor orphan boy who survived on the charity of his benefactor at the sutler's store. He couldn't possibly pose a threat to anyone.

When the major insisted he needed proof, Kane referred him to the discovery of the fresh-minted gold coins in Curly Smith's saddle-bags at the time of his arrest in town.

'The coins didn't belong to Curly, they belonged to the kid,' he insisted. 'Curly borrowed Miguel's pony when he rode into town that evening, his own mount had thrown a shoe. He told me he literally hopped into the saddle the second the kid entered the compound. The saddle-bags were Miguel's, which means the sack of coins must have been his too. Now you tell me how a boy of his age came by so much money?'

'So you reckon it was payment from his Comanchero masters?'

'That's exactly what I think. And I wouldn't mind betting that somewhere in his personables we'll find a few more sacks of coins stashed away.'

'What do you propose to do?' asked Turner, resting his elbows on the desk before him.

'I'm gonna haul his young ass in here and nail his hide to the wall,' promised Kane.

'Then you'd better go fetch him,' said Turner, with just the ghost of a smile.

The sutler's store was deserted, save for the owner, Fernando Juárez, when Kane sauntered in through the door. The Mexican was in the process of restocking the main shelf directly behind the trestled counter. He turned to face his visitor, hands full of tins of beans.

'Where's Miguel?' asked Kane.

'What do you want with him?' replied the store-keeper, placing the cans of beans on the counter in front of him.

'That's my business,' insisted the scout. 'Now where is he?'

'He ain't here,' said Juárez, nervously licking his lips. 'As a matter of fact, I haven't seen hide nor hair of him for days. He pretty much comes and goes as he damn well pleases, which is why I'm having to fill my own shelves. Is he in some sort of trouble?'

'You could say that,' said Kane. 'Do you have any idea where he went?'

The trader shook his head.

'Never mind, I reckon I might just know where to look.' With that, the scout turned on his heels and made for the door.

Turner wasn't at all sure he liked the idea of Kane chasing half-way across the territory in search of the missing orphan, not when they still had a killer on the loose. When he said as much, his scout insisted he knew what he was doing.

'There could still be more to this than meets the eye,' he said, moving towards the door. 'Others could be involved in the gun-running and until we talk to the kid we can't be sure. If I leave right away, I should make it to Jasper and back by the day after tomorrow.'

'And what do we do in the meantime?' Kane smiled.

'Keep a close eye on all the members of our patrol, make sure none of them leaves the post and interrogate them individually to see if they know anything.'

'Look out for your top-knot, Sam, don't underesti-
mate that little Mexican, your death might prove a
little inconvenient right now,' offered Turner, as
Kane left his office.

The shot which rang out through the still night air
as he shut the door behind him missed his head by
inches. He dived headlong to the ground, losing his
hat in the process, as a second shot exploded out of
the darkness. It sent dust and shards of adobe brick
flying into the air as it struck the front wall of the
building. Kane rolled over and over in the dirt until
he was able to find shelter behind a nearby water
trough. He tried to work out where the shots had
come from, but in spite of the bright moon, much of
the compound remained cloaked in shadow. All
about him people were running to the scene to see
what all the fuss was about. He heard the duty officer
loudly demand an explanation for all the shooting
from the doorway of the post adjutant's office.
Turner appeared at his shoulder as he stood up and
holstered his gun.

'What the hell happened, Sam?'

'Our killer just decided to have another go at
adding me to his list of victims.'

'Did you see anything?'

Kane shook his head, then reclaimed his hat.

'No, not a thing. The shots could have come from
anywhere, I didn't see so much as a muzzle-flash. But
I reckon our killer might just have given himself
away.'

'How do you work that out?' queried the major.
'You just said you didn't see him.'

'I didn't need to,' advised Kane. 'Whoever it was, they must have snuck out of the barracks they were confined to in order to take their pot shots at me. Someone will have noticed their absence, so let's go talk to the members of our patrol and see who is unaccounted for.'

'I'm right with you,' agreed the major, 'but let's get some help, there's no point in taking any chances.'

Turner shouted for the duty officer to report directly to him with two troopers. He then reassured all the concerned onlookers that everything was all right. The crowd gradually began to disperse, muttering to each other. Within seconds, Lieutenant Ratcliffe appeared at Turner's side, accompanied by a pair of armed sentries. Without bothering to explain, the major led the way towards the low barracks room where the troopers who had done battle with the Comancheros were resting. By the time they arrived, a bleary-eyed Dick Squires had joined them. Kane quickly filled him in on what had happened.

On entering the barracks, they found all the troopers to be wide awake. Most of them were either lying or sitting on their bunks in various stages of undress, generally relaxing, while a few were gathered around the table at the far end of the room, playing cards. All eyes turned towards their commanding officer as he halted just inside the battered, squeaky door.

'Have any of you men left the barracks in the past few minutes?' he barked, his eyes sweeping the room for any sign of guilt on the troopers' faces. There were muttered nos and much shaking of heads, then Gimenez spoke up from his seat at the card-table.

'Pat Halliday went out a while back to use the latrine.'

'Yeah,' agreed Jake Faraday, swinging his legs over the side of his bunk to face the newcomers, 'and he ain't come back yet.'

Turner nodded towards Kane. 'Looks like Halliday's our man,' he said. 'Let's go find him.' He swung about to face the two armed sentries. 'One of you stay here; no one else is to leave the barracks tonight for any reason unless you get clearance from me personally.'

The private closest to the major nodded and moved to take up station by the door. The rest of the party turned on their heels and went out into the warm night air.

Kane placed a restraining hand on the major's shoulder to halt his angry, determined march across the parade ground towards the company latrines. Even in the dark, Turner could recognize doubt in the scout's eyes. Something was troubling him.

'What is it?' he asked, keeping his voice low.

'I know Pat Halliday,' said Kane. 'He's a damn fine trooper, they don't come any better. I don't reckon he's our man.'

'But he's the only one who left the barracks, and he's also unaccounted for.'

'I'll grant you things look bad for him right now,' agreed Kane, 'but I still can't figure him for our killer. York and Gannon were his two best friends in all the world. They rode through hell together on many an occasion. Why would he kill them?'

'That's just what I aim to ask when we find him,' insisted the major, setting off once more towards the far side of the eerily lit compound.

They were half-way to the latrines when they sited a shadowy figure stumbling in ungainly fashion towards them. Although he couldn't see his face, the man's build and height told Kane they had located their quarry. He called out a request for the faltering figure to confirm his identity. When the man did so, the sentry at Turner's side raised his Springfield rifle to cover him.

'Is that you, Kane?' queried Halliday, as he almost stumbled into the scout's arms.

'Are you drunk, Halliday?' demanded Turner, with an air of disgust.

'No, sir,' insisted the trooper, who seemed genuinely unstable on his feet. With a determined effort, he managed to stand upright without support. 'Someone clubbed me across the back of the head when I went into the latrines.' He gave the back of his head a rub.

'Take his sidearm,' ordered the major.

Dick Squires stepped forward to remove the trooper's Navy Colt from the flapped holster on his hip. He put the barrel to his nose, sniffed deeply, nodded, then checked the cylindrical magazine before shaking his head in disgust.

'It's been fired recently,' he announced. 'The barrel's still warm and there are two spent cartridge cases in the cylinder. Looks like we've got our man.'

Kane sighed deeply and shook his head sadly.

'I never figured you for a cold-blooded killer, Pat,' he said. 'Why'd you do it?'

'That's what I'd like to know,' interjected Turner.

'Do what?' queried Halliday, with a puzzled frown. 'I ain't got any idea what y'all are talking about.'

'Sure you do,' insisted the major, 'so stop putting on an act. You just tried to kill Sam, though I can't for the life of me begin to understand why. But I guess you must have had your reasons, just as you had for killing Rothwell, York and Gannon.'

Halliday shook his head, his slightly glazed eyes dancing from face to face.

'I didn't kill no one!' he exclaimed. 'I told y'all, someone snuck up behind me and knocked me on the head. Whoever it was, he must have taken my gun.'

'Now that just seems a mite too convenient,' stated his commanding officer. He glanced towards the sentry at his side and nodded towards the shaken figure of Halliday. 'Take him away,' he barked. 'I'll interrogate him properly in the morning.'

The unhappy trooper was still animatedly protesting his innocence as he was escorted away to spend the night in the guardhouse. Kane folded his left arm across his chest and took hold of his bristly chin with his right hand. He was so deep in thought he failed to appreciate that Turner was talking to him.

'Huh?' he said, when the major finally managed to gain his attention.

'I was just saying that I'm glad the matter's been resolved.'

'I'm not so sure it has,' Kane argued.

'But the evidence says otherwise,' insisted Turner, happily. 'Halliday had the opportunity; after all, he was present when each of the men was killed.'

'I cain't argue with you on that,' agreed Kane. 'But what motive could he possibly have for murdering three of his fellow troopers? Two of whom were known to be his closest pals.'

'I don't know,' conceded the major. 'But he was caught red-handed with a smoking gun, and that's enough to convince me we have the right man. As for his motive, it will probably come out at his court martial.'

'Maybe so,' conceded Kane.

A split second later an animated, startled cry echoed through the night from the direction of the guardhouse. The two scouts instinctively drew their sidearms as they took to their heels to investigate the unexpected disturbance on the other side of the compound. On their arrival they found the sentry and Halliday staring in disbelief at the smashed lock and open door to the empty cell which had previously contained the Comanchero prisoner.

'Just what the hell's going on around here, Sam?' asked a baffled Turner.

'I'm darned if I know!' replied the scout. 'But I sure aim to find out.'

The major turned to face a breathless Lieutenant Ratcliffe, who had just arrived belatedly on the scene in response to the sentry's call.

'Get the locksmith out of bed,' he ordered. 'I want the door fixed immediately and Halliday secured.

Until then, he is to remain under armed guard in the adjutant's office.'

'Yes, sir,' replied a harassed and embarrassed-looking Ratcliffe.

'I also want six troopers to mount a search for our missing Comanchero,' added Turner, as an afterthought.

'Don't waste your time,' sighed Kane. 'He's long gone. Besides, I reckon I'll catch up with him when I go after little Miguel.'

'You think they're both heading for Jasper?'

Kane nodded.

'OK. Lieutenant Ratcliffe, get Halliday out of here,' said Turner.

'You seem to have all the fun on your watch, Lieutenant!' joked Dick Squires. Ratcliffe scowled at the scout, before leaving in a huff, cursing under his breath.

'Are you leaving at first light?' asked Turner, as Kane started to move away in the direction of the scout's quarters with Squires at his side.

He shook his head. 'I'm aiming to leave right now.'

'In the middle of the night?'

The scout nodded.

'But you must be exhausted from your ride to Garston Crossing?'

'They'll be plenty of time for sleep once I've had me a talk with little Miguel,' insisted Kane. 'Mano's escape tonight would seem to suggest that someone else at the fort is working with the kid. I aim to find out who it is.'

'Are you going with him?' asked Turner, nodding towards Dick Squires.

'No he ain't!' said Kane. 'He's staying put. I ain't as convinced as you are that Halliday's our killer, so I'll be a whole lot happier if Dick stays around to keep an eye on things.'

'Have it your way,' sighed Turner, waving him on his way dismissively.

Kane rode through the night until his tired mind and body told him he could go no further. He dismounted beneath the waning moon and led his mount down a steep incline into the bottom of a dry wash. Having unsaddled and tethered his pony, he spread his blanket out on the sandy ground, intent on snatching a few hours' sleep before continuing his journey come daybreak.

He was awake at first light, some sixth sense warning him that all was not well. As he lay still, hat pulled down over his eyes, maintaining an illusion of sleep, he listened for any discordant sound. Within seconds the almost imperceptible scraping of a boot over loose pebbles near by told him all he needed to know. Someone was stalking him from above, a fact confirmed by the skittish snorting of his pony. Quick as a flash, he pulled his hat clear of his eyes, discarded his blanket, grabbed the pistol lying by his side and came to his feet, primed for action.

As his would-be assailant appeared at the top of the bank directly above him, shotgun in hand, Kane fired twice from the hip. The man never stood a chance. Both bullets caught him flush in the chest, causing him to drop his own weapon. For a moment he stared incredulously at the rapidly spreading dark stain in his checked shirt, then toppled head first into the wash. Kane stepped aside in the nick of time as the lifeless body of Fernando Juárez fell face down in the sand right where he had been standing.

'Well I guess that sure as hell tells me who little Miguel's contact was at the fort,' he said, shaking his head. 'I never did take to you, Señor Juárez, now I know why!'

XII

Jasper was truly the quintessential Texas frontier settlement: small, dusty, windswept, insignificant and interminably dull as far as the poor, hard-working white and Hispanic souls who called it home were concerned. It nestled up against the northern bank of the narrow, shallow, leisurely flowing river that shared its name, in a broad expanse of treeless (save for the cottonwoods close to the water's edge) grassy highplain, half a day's ride south-west of Fort Walsh. Numerous small, struggling ranches and dirt-poor farms, all dependent upon the river, lay round about. Their owners carved out a hard, precarious way of life on the sun-baked prairie, where they were constantly afflicted by the unrelenting elements as well as bugs of all shapes and sizes; disease and, occasionally, during the Comanche moon, small raiding parties whose primary target was the livestock.

A tiny, cramped, white-walled stone church, complete with bell-tower, stood proud and defiant close to the river. It was the oldest structure in town, having originally been built by a band of Franciscan monks, keen to spread the Christian message amongst the various Indian bands who roamed the wilderness. They left for pastures new within a few years, having failed to attract a single convert from the wary, superstitious native population. The town that ultimately sprang up around the dilapidated church owed its origins to a Kentucky family who arrived in the region soon after the Texan war of independence. Others soon followed.

Adobe was the popular choice of building material in Jasper. Only the wooden, creosoted façade of the general store-cum-saloon-cum-barbershop bucked the trend. It was located in the centre of town, between the undertaker's and the pharmacy. Directly opposite, on the other side of the one and only street, stood a small schoolhouse, a livery stable, a carpenter's shop and a half-dozen wind-battered, single-storeyed, ramshackle dwellings. It was here, following a hunch, that Kane came in search of the runaway orphan, Miguel Diaz.

He arrived around noon, fully aware that towns such as Jasper rarely saw visitors and that his presence would probably be greeted with grave suspicion by the local inhabitants. His dusty, grimy, unshaven countenance was likely to have any lawman worth his salt checking his Wanted posters. But as far as he was aware, the town didn't have its own serving peace officer, nor, in truth, did it have any need for one. The locals were an easy-going, self-regulating bunch. Disputes between themselves were rare and the settlement was far too poor to attract the attention of any of the notorious bands of post-Civil War outlaws, former Confederate soldiers, guerrillas and other social misfits, who robbed banks and stagecoaches for a living. The infrequent but welcome Ranger patrols gave them a sense of security, especially when it came to providing intelligence about Indian raids during the period of the Comanche moon, always a dangerous time of year for any isolated settlement.

Kane was perfectly capable of looking out for himself, even in the roughest company, so his main concern was that when he started asking around, the Hispanics would close ranks to protect the orphan he sought. If he was right about the kid heading for Jasper, a conclusion he had reached based on Mano's comments about the town being a rendezvous for Chico and his contact at the fort, he had to run him to ground quickly before the young renegade knew he was there.

The dusty, rutted street was totally deserted when he entered the quiet settlement. He rode slowly towards the general store, his eyes surreptitiously scanning every door and window he passed. He reined in by the hitching post in front of the general store and dismounted, flexing his stiff leg, wondering if the knife-wound he had suffered months earlier during a nearly fatal run-in with the Comanches was destined to bother him for the rest of his life. His thoughts inevitably drifted to young Daniel, who had been a part of that particular adventure. He hoped the boy was happy now that he was back at the Davies ranch under the protection of two females of different ages, who both adored him equally.

The tinkling of a bell strategically positioned above the door of the store brought him out of his reverie. He looked up into the unsmiling face of a middle-aged white woman in a dark-blue gingham dress who was making her way haughtily down the three narrow wooden steps towards him. She carried a shopping-basket full of groceries in her left hand and a brown-paper package in her right. He tipped his hat and bade her good-day as she swept past him with a glare designed to cut him to the quick. At least it confirmed his gut feeling that the good citizens of Jasper were likely to be anything but friendly towards a trail-weary stranger. With a rueful grin and shake of his head, he trotted up the steps and on inside the store to question the proprietor.

The melodic chimes of the bell announced his presence to the storekeeper, who had his broad back turned to him, counting stock on a rear shelf, when he entered the large, stuffy room. Every last nook and cranny was crammed full of goods of all sorts: barrels of fresh produce, bales of cloth, sacks of flour, saddles and bridles, ropes, shelves filled to bursting with jars of hard boiled sweets and tin cans, even a glass display-cabinet loaded with various types of handguns. On the wall directly behind, was a rack of rifles, some obviously brand new, others second hand.

'Can I help you, mister?' asked the rotund, balding, storekeeper as he turned to face Kane. The tone of his voice was friendly enough, but there was no welcoming smile, just a curious stare as he gave his newly arrived customer the once-over.

'I sure hope so,' replied the scout, placing his hands wide apart on the counter. 'The name's Kane, Sam Kane. I'm an army scout, based at Fort Walsh.'

'You have my sympathy,' remarked his host, maintaining a deadpan expression. 'My name's Joel Wilkins and I own this place. Now what can I get you?'

'I'm after some information,' stated the scout, holding his ground.

'It's about the only thing I don't sell,' replied Wilkins, placing his thumbs in the cord tied around his white, sleeveless apron. 'Out here it pays a man to mind his own business, so there ain't nothing I can tell you about anything or anybody, scout. Close the door on your way out.' With that, he turned away to resume his stocktaking.

'I was afraid you might decide to be difficult,' said Kane with a sigh. His right hand instantly snaked out to grab hold of the man by the sleeve of his checked shirt, causing him to spin around on his heels with a nimbleness that belied his heavy build.

'Let go before I break your arm!' hissed the storekeeper, flexing his own muscular limb. 'I've eaten bigger things than you for breakfast.'

'I ain't looking for trouble,' insisted Kane, his eyes narrowing. He tightened his grip on the angry man's arm, 'but nor am I in the mood to take any crap from a two-bit storekeeper! Now, I'm looking for a no-good son of a bitch who has been selling guns to the Comanches, and the trail has led me right here to your door.'

'I ain't no renegade!' roared a red-faced Wilkins,

desperately trying to pull away from the scout's vice-like grip, genuinely surprised by the change in his visitor's easy-going countenance as well as his physical strength. 'I hate the stinking Comanche as much as the next man.'

'Then answer my questions.'

The man thought things over for a moment, then nodded slowly. Kane relinquished his hold on the man's arm and placed his hands back on the counter, maintaining his implacable, unblinking stare. Not for the first time in his life he had successfully spooked a man much larger and possibly physically stronger than himself. But when it came to pure kick-ass meanness, size wasn't everything! It took a lot to get Kane mad, but when he lost his temper, the luck-less few who had the misfortune to upset him generally counted the cost in terms of broken bones, lost teeth and numerous bruises. The storekeeper was sweating profusely. He knew he had met his match and was now fully prepared to tell the stranger what ever it was he wanted to know, in order to be rid of him.

'I'm looking for a young Mexican boy, name of Miguel Diaz,' stated Kane.

'I've never heard of him,' replied Wilkins, 'God's honest truth, mister.'

'The kid looks about thirteen. He's about four foot six, skinny with brown eyes and jet-black hair.'

'That description would fit any number of kids who live around here.'

'He don't actually live in Jasper,' advised Kane. 'At least not nowadays, though he might well have done, up until about a year ago. But he could have kin here.'

The storekeeper shrugged his shoulders.

'The Mexicans don't frequent my store all that much,' he replied, 'and as I don't exactly spend much time socializing with them, I wouldn't know too much about their business. They breed like rabbits and all look much the same to me, so I really wouldn't notice if one of them upped stakes and left.'

'The boy also has a small, jagged scar on his cheek, just below his left ear.'

The storekeeper's eyes suddenly lit up.

'You could be talking about Juan Dominguez's boy Raol. Come to think of it, he don't seem to be around much these days.' He quickly told Kane where he could find the Dominguez farm, which lay but a short distance outside of town. 'You can't miss it, the house has bright-red shutters on the windows,' he said.

To Wilkins's immense relief, the scout thanked him for his help and swiftly took his leave. However, the storekeeper didn't fully relax until he heard his unwelcome visitor's horse cantering away in the direction of the river. He debated whether it might make sense to close up for the rest of the day, in case the scout returned, but he thought better of it. After all, Sam Kane had not struck him as the sort of man who would be deterred by the simple matter of a locked door.

Kane forded the river and headed due south at a canter, following a well-worn trail towards a cluster of low white farm buildings. As he drew closer, he could plainly see red shutters on the windows of a house just off to his left. He rode on up to the rickety old fence that surrounded the traditional, peon-style, single-storey home much favoured by the dirt-poor Mexicans on both sides of the border, and surveyed the scene. As well as the adobe house there was a pigpen, a chicken coop and a lean-to shelter, which contained a donkey and a pair of horses, one of which the scout recognized as belonging to Miguel Diaz, or whatever his real name might be. The other animal carried the brand of the US Cavalry. Two saddles lay discarded on the straw-covered floor close by. Without moment's hesitation, he grabbed his Winchester, swiftly dismounted and entered the yard through the five-barred gate directly in front of him.

A handful of chickens clucked loudly and scampered out of his way as he crossed the yard. Half-way to the house he stopped dead in his tracks as the front door swung open. A short, thin, wiry Mexican farmer, dressed all in white stepped out to greet him, rifle in hand.

'That is far enough, *amigo*,' he stated, pointing his weapon at Kane's midriff. 'Lay your Winchester on the ground and then unbuckle your gun belt.'

'I don't think I can rightly do that!' replied Kane, whose own rifle had swung up to cover the door the moment he heard it creak open.

'What do you want here?' demanded his unsmiling host.

'I wish to speak to the owners of the horses you have stabled in your lean-to,' replied the scout, suddenly noticing a rifle barrel sticking out of the window nearest to the door. 'Come on out, Mano, don't be shy.' The gun was instantly withdrawn and a moment later the Comanchero appeared at the farmer's side.

'*Buenas tardes*, Señor Kane,' he said. 'It is a pleasure to see you again, for it gives me the perfect opportunity to avenge my friends.'

'You ain't good enough!' insisted Kane, keeping a watchful eye on both of the men standing before him. 'But I tell you what, answer all my questions and then maybe I might just let y'all live.'

'Go to hell, gringo!' snarled the Comanchero, raising his rifle.

Kane fired from the hip, his bullet tearing into Mano's heart before the Comanchero could even shoulder his gun. Kane instinctively dropped to one knee and fired again as the farmer belatedly drew a bead on the lightning-fast scout. Kane's second bullet hit the Mexican squarely between the eyes, killing him instantly as he toppled backwards like a felled log. He lay spread-eagled on the dusty ground, blood flowing liberally from his head, eyes fully open, but glazed over, shock etched on his weather-beaten face.

In the nick of time, the tell-tale click of a pistol hammer being cocked warned Kane of a new threat inside the house. He rolled over and over in the dirt a split second before a bullet sent a puff of dust high into the air at the very spot where he had been kneeling, silently cursing the fact that he had killed both the Mexicans outright before he had had a chance to question them. A second shot tore a neat hole in the sleeve of his buckskin jacket as he lay on the ground, trying to locate the hidden gunman. He instantly jumped to his feet and dived for cover behind the dilapidated lean-to.

A third bullet pinged into the wall, inches above his head, as he peered around the corner of the building, sending shards of dried adobe spinning high into the air. As he ducked back out of harm's way he caught sight of a bobbing head in the window furthest from the door. He took a deep breath to steady himself, shouldered his rifle and came to his feet, firing as he stepped out from around the corner of the lean-to. The four bullets he sent winging through the open window kept his assailant pinned down as he sprinted for the door and burst inside the house.

'Drop it!' he yelled at the figure kneeling beside the window, as he shouldered his Winchester. 'Don't make me shoot you, boy!'

Although the youngster he knew as Miguel Diaz nodded and at first lowered his pistol, something about the kid's body-language suggested he did not have surrender in mind. Sure enough, as the boy slowly stood up he suddenly brought his gun to bear on the scout. Not for the first time, Kane's lightning-fast reactions saved his life. He fired without aiming the second he saw the boy's pistol swing up. His bullet caught the young renegade in the stomach. The boy instantly dropped his pistol, crying out in agony and shock, as he collapsed to his knees. There he rocked back and forth, wailing pitifully, hands clasped over the gaping wound in his belly, blood seeping out from between his clenched fingers.

Kane cursed loudly, shook his head and leaned his rifle up against the wall. He slowly advanced towards the stricken youngster. The boy gritted his teeth in response to a wicked spasm of pain in his belly as the scout gently eased his blood-covered hands out of the way in order to get a proper view of the wound.

'It's bad, isn't it?' said the youngster through his tears.

'It sure ain't good, kid,' admitted Kane. He removed the bandanna from around his neck and stuffed it into the hole in the boy's stomach. 'We need to get you to a doctor.'

'No!' exclaimed the boy, doubling up with pain. 'Please don't move me. It hurts too much. Just let me stay here.'

'OK,' agreed Kane, draping a supportive arm around the boy's slender, bony shoulders. The boy's whole body convulsed with pain. Blood appeared at the corner of his pale mouth. He was in bad shape. Kane knew he was dying in his arms.

'How come you got involved with such a bad bunch?' he asked, wiping the youngster's sweaty brow with the palm of his hand.

Miguel Diaz coughed again. More blood seeped from the corner of his mouth. He closed his eyes for a second in response to the burning sensation in his belly. When he opened them again he stared up into the sad face of the scout and slowly shook his head.

'I didn't have any choice,' he said. 'My papa was a Comanchero. You killed him, Mano told me all about it. But I don't hate you for it, you were only doing what you had to, gringo. And at least like me, Papa died with a gun in his hand, and not at the end of a rope.'

'Who was your papa, boy?'

'Chico Morales,' he said, fighting to catch his breath. 'He was a legend, the greatest of the *pistoleros*, all men feared him. You must have tricked him when you killed him, no man could face him in a fair fight and live.'

'You called it right, kid,' said Kane, not wishing to shatter the boy's illusions at the moment of his passing. 'I shot him when he wasn't looking. Had to, 'twas the only way I could get the better of him.'

'I knew it,' sighed the youngster.

'So is your name really Miguel?'

The boy nodded. 'Miguel Elvarez Pedro Antonio Morales,' he said, proudly. 'But most people round here know me as Raol Dominguez. My uncle owns this farm, at least he did until you killed him. I lived here as his son from the time my mother died eight years ago.'

'Just another link in the chain,' remarked Kane.

'Pardon, *señor*?' queried young Miguel, his voice growing weaker by the minute.

'Nothing,' replied Kane. ' 'Twas nothing. And Juárez was your contact at the fort?'

'What do you mean?' queried the youngster. He groaned loudly and hugged his belly tightly as another awful spasm of pain shot through his insides.

'He was the one who helped you to get the information you needed for your papa?'

'I'm saying nothing,' sighed Miguel.

Kane shook his head. 'You don't have to,' advised the scout. 'Your pal tried to ambush me on the way here.'

'Then you know everything,' said the boy.

'Almost,' replied Kane, as Miguel Morales gave one last rasping cough. The boy closed his eyes and sagged back limply into the scout's cushioning arms.

'God damn!' snarled Kane, gently lowering the boy to the floor.

He climbed to his feet, retrieved his Winchester from its resting place against the wall and moved towards the door. He felt sorely in need of some fresh air to clear his head, but as he stepped outside into the glare of the sun he came face to face with a dozen peon farmers armed to the teeth with deadly machetes and wicked-looking knives.

'There's been enough killing here today,' he said calmly, chambering a fresh round into his rifle. 'These *bandidos* got what they deserved. You'd be better off burying them rather than joining them!'

The peon at the front of the crowd lowered his machete and nodded. The others instantly followed suit. They backed slowly and sullenly away to the side, clearing a path for him as he strolled towards the gate. He replaced his Winchester in his saddle boot, quickly mounted his horse and rode off in the direction of Fort Walsh without so much as a backward glance.

XIII

Kane stirred from a fitful sleep as the company bugler sounded reveille. Weary and bleary-eyed, having returned to the post just a few hours earlier, he rose from his cot, stretching tight and aching muscles, and pulled on his boots. He could easily have slept on, but proper rest would have to wait, for he needed to confer with the major about what had happened during his visit to Jasper. He also wanted to talk with Pat Halliday.

Despite the evidence to the contrary, the scout still didn't believe the trooper was responsible for the attempt on his life, nor for the cold-blooded murder of his former comrades in arms. It just did not add up. What possible reason could he have had for wanting Kane or his friends dead? No, it was much more likely he had, as he claimed, been knocked out when he entered the latrines, his gun used to make him look guilty.

Kane found the major seated behind his desk in the headquarters building, deep in conversation with Captain Cummings and Lieutenant Ratcliffe, looking anything but happy. He immediately sensed something had happened in his absence.

'Glad to see you back, Sam,' said Turner, beckoning him to take a seat next to an unsmiling Lieutenant Ratcliffe. 'How did it go?'

Kane quickly provided his subdued audience with a concise report, sticking purely to the facts as he saw them. They listened intently, without interruption. Although he did not openly express remorse over the sad demise of Miguel, Turner could tell by the slight tremble in his voice and the pained expression on his face that the scout was troubled by it.

'Well, at least we now know why Juárez vanished from the post so mysteriously,' said Turner, when the scout had completed his account. 'But why do you think he came after you, Sam?'

Kane shrugged his shoulders. 'He probably figured Miguel would talk once I caught up with him.'

'And now we have to make arrangements to find another post trader.'

'We also have a killer to track down.'

'No we don't,' corrected Turner, impassively. 'We've got our killer.'

'You mean Halliday.'

The major nodded.

'I don't agree,' said Kane stubbornly, shaking his head. 'No, sir, it just can't be.'

When Turner asked him why he was so certain Halliday was not the guilty party, the scout insisted it simply didn't make a lick of sense.

'But he was the only trooper missing from the

barracks at the time of the attack on you,' stated Captain Cummings.

'And he was almost caught with a smoking gun in his hand,' added Ratcliffe. 'That makes him look mighty guilty in my book.'

'Not in mine,' argued the scout. 'What if he was clubbed on the back of the head as he claimed? Whoever done it could then have used Halliday's gun to try and kill me, leaving him to shoulder the blame.'

'That's fanciful eye wash and you know it!' exclaimed Cummings.

'With all due respect, Sam,' interjected Ratcliffe, 'I tend to agree with Captain Cummings. You're clutching at straws.'

'Am I? Then tell me this; what possible motive could he have for killing his two best friends and trying to do the same to me?'

'That's something we'll never have a chance to ask him,' said Turner.

'What do you mean?' queried Kane, frowning. Turner sighed deeply. 'Halliday committed suicide the night you left for Jasper.'

'He hanged himself with his own belt from the bars of his cell window,' said Ratcliffe.

'The cowardly backstabber couldn't face the disgrace of a court martial,' interjected Cummings, his loathing for the dead man all too clear from the tone of his voice.

Kane shook his head and cursed under his breath.

'It all seems a mite too convenient for my liking,' he growled. 'We find him with a gun in his hand, he tells us someone clumped him on the head and the same night he decides the game's up so he goes and hangs himself. I don't like the smell of this one little bit.'

'An innocent man would not have taken his own life,' insisted Cummings.

Kane kept shaking his head. He just could not accept what they were saying. The popular, fun-loving, hard-drinking, hard-riding Halliday was a man he would have trusted with his life. He was above all else a fighter, not the sort of man who would ever take the easy way out, even if he had been guilty of the murders. Suicide would not have been an option; he would more likely have tried to escape. In spite of the evidence and the undeniable fact that Halliday had indeed had the opportunity to carry out each of the crimes for which he stood accused, Kane sensed they were barking up the wrong tree.

'Are you sure Halliday committed suicide?' he asked, fidgeting uncomfortably in his seat.

'Of course!' exclaimed Cummings, irritably. 'The guard found him dangling from the bars in the window of his cell just after reveille.'

'Were there any marks on his body?'

'Yeah,' said Ratcliffe, 'a red-and-blue weal around his neck where the belt strangled the life out of him.'

'Any other bruises or wounds of any kind?'

The lieutenant shrugged his shoulders. 'I wouldn't know.'

'I doubt if anyone even bothered looking,' offered Cummings. 'After all, the cause of death was all too obvious.'

'Then I suggest we go take a look-see right now,' suggested Kane, calmly.

The three officers looked at him, aghast. Once he had got over his sense of shock, Turner demanded to know if he was joking, but the scout assured him he was not. He stubbornly restated his opinion that Halliday's death was rather too convenient.

'So what good will viewing the body do?' Cummings asked, incredulously.

'Probably none,' conceded Kane. 'But I'd still like to take a gander.'

'It's a complete waste of time!' roared Cummings, coming to his feet. 'Tell this scout to return to his duties and let us get back to ours.'

The major put his hand up to silence his second in command. Turner had great respect for the scout and generally trusted his instincts implicitly. If Kane had something stuck in his craw about this business then he was quite prepared to see him play out his hand. He looked him directly in the eye and gave an almost imperceptible nod.

'OK,' he said, 'have it your way. Halliday was interred almost immediately, so I guess we'll just have to dig him up for you.'

Within the hour the three officers and Kane, accompanied by two enlisted men, who were to do the digging, gathered in the small cemetery outside the main compound to exhume the body of trooper Halliday. The privates toiled manfully and silently beneath the burning sun for the best part of twenty minutes to complete their distasteful task. An intrigued-looking Dick Squires arrived on the scene

130

just as the heavy white-cotton shroud containing the corpse was hauled out of the grave. He frowned at his friend, but kept his own counsel.

'Didn't he warrant a proper wooden casket?' sighed Kane, stepping forward to run his knife down the stitched seam that ran the length of the sacking.

'He was a murderer,' hissed Captain Cummings, dismissively. 'If I'd had my way, he'd have been left to the buzzards.'

The scout replaced the knife in his belt and pulled back the neatly split canvas to reveal the pallid body, which was dressed only in army-issue long johns. Trying his best to ignore the overpowering stench of death, he knelt down beside the corpse. The first thing he noticed was the vivid red-and-blue marks about the neck. It was exactly what he had expected to find, given what he had been told about the man's death. However, what he did find surprising, although at first he kept it to himself, was the fact that Halliday's head was lolling to one side. On closer inspection he could see that the man's neck was broken.

Kane frowned. He knew for certain that the barred window in the cell was no more than eight feet above the floor. Allowing for the length of the belt and his own height, Halliday could only have dropped a matter of a foot or so, not far enough to have snapped his neck. By rights he should have choked to death.

As reverently as possible, he carefully rolled the corpse over on to its back, noticing immediately the small lump and congealed blood on the back of the head. This was further evidence that all was not what it seemed.

'I think we need some privacy, Major,' he said, standing up and nodding towards the dusty, sweat-sodden troopers who were leaning on their shovels beside the open grave.

Turner duly ordered the enlisted men to return to their barracks. For their part, the two troopers were only too pleased to take their leave of the cemetery and wasted no time in making themselves scarce. Once they were out of earshot, Kane revealed his findings to his visibly stunned companions.

'Are you sure about all this, Sam?' sighed Turner.

Kane nodded. 'I'm certain,' he said, 'but don't just take my word for it, take a look for yourself. The evidence is plain to see. He was hit on the head from behind. His killer then broke his neck and strung him up by his belt to make it look as if he took his own life.'

'Then the killer must still be at large,' stated Lieutenant Ratcliffe.

'That he is,' agreed Kane. 'Which is precisely why I wanted to hold this discussion in private. If the troopers catch wind of this we'll most likely cause a panic in the ranks.'

'We need to find this mean son of a bitch,' said Squires, spitting out a chaw of dark tobacco. 'And quickly, before he kills again!'

Turner swung round to face Cummings and Ratcliffe.

'Captain, have the bugler sound officers' call. I'll

meet you at headquarters in ten minutes.'

Cummings saluted and left without comment or delay. Ratcliffe was instructed to have Halliday's body transferred to the infirmary, until such time as a proper funeral, one befitting that of a cavalryman, could be arranged.

'Who can be doing this?' asked Turner, when at last he was alone with the scouts. Kane shrugged his shoulders as Squires dropped to one knee to roll Halliday gently over on to his back.

'I don't know,' he replied, moving away towards the white picket fence which bordered the cemetery, 'but I'm gonna flush him out if it's the last thing I do, you have my word on it.'

'Where are you going?'

Kane halted, swung back to face the major and informed him he was headed for Miller Springs. When Turner asked why, the scout replied that he wanted to try to learn more about the first to die, the unidentified stranger in town.

'So you don't think Curly Smith did it?' asked the major.

'No,' replied Kane. 'Curly told me he didn't do it, and I happen to believe him. In which case, all the killings must be linked in some way.'

'OK,' conceded the major. 'You could be right.'

'Curly didn't have any extra set of duds in his belongings when he was arrested, which also convinces me he was set up to take the fall for someone else.'

'So why was the stranger stripped and disfigured by the killer?' queried the major.

'To prevent anyone in town from identifying the body,' said Kane.

'Precisely,' agreed Squires, nodding in approval of his friend's logic. 'Whoever he was, the chances are someone in town saw him before he died, and they might have recognized him and remembered his name, if'n the killer hadn't messed up his face.'

'Watch your back, Sam,' called the major as Kane moved away.

'I won't need to,' Kane replied. 'That's Dick's job!'

'It is?' queried his friend.

'It is,' insisted Kane, beckoning him to join him. 'Now, let's get a move on. I want to be there and back before nightfall.'

XIV

As was their wont, the scouts maintained a watchful silence as they rode the well-worn, dusty trail into Miller Springs. The sun blazed down out of a cloud-less sky without the merest hint of a cooling breeze to bring relief from either the sticky, oppressive humidity or the winged insects which dogged their path. However, apart from the midges and flies, they never caught sight of another living creature on their uneventful and tediously hot trek into town.

Although he kept his wits about him, Kane spent much of the time dwelling on the events which had necessitated their journey. He kept going over and over everything that had happened since he and Daniel had returned from their fruitless sojourn to Missouri. Counting the stranger in town, six men had been murdered, and he was still no nearer identify-ing the killer, or establishing any sort of a motive for the crimes. However, he was utterly convinced the deaths were all linked, that there was a pattern, even if it still frustratingly eluded him.

In one respect, the scout felt lucky, for he too could easily have fallen foul of the faceless assassin. Twice the murderer had tried to gun him down from ambush, only narrowly to fail. It was this that he found the most puzzling. He had already spent many a long hour trying to figure out who on the post might have reason to see him dead, and why.

Sam Kane was a private man who kept himself to himself. He had few close friends, but called no man his enemy, save for the Comanches and their Comanchero allies. If he was on the killer's death list, and the attempts on his life certainly appeared to confirm it, then he must have had something in common with the other victims. But what? No matter how hard he racked his brain, he just could not figure it out.

'Danged if I can make sense of it,' he muttered, shaking his head in frustration.

'What was that, pard?' questioned his companion.

'Nothing,' replied Kane. 'I was just thinking out loud.'

Silence enveloped them once more as they rode on through the shimmering heat of the day. Kane immediately returned to his private battle to make sense of things. He tried to focus his thoughts on the successful mission to recover the guns from the Comancheros. It was during their time in hostile country that he had first become aware of the presence of a killer in their midst. Three men had died and he himself had missed a similar fate by a cat's whisker. Surely the murderer must have made a mistake somewhere along the way? Could he possibly be missing something? Was he ignoring some vital clue that would expose the man in the shadows? He felt the answer was there somewhere, tantalizingly staring him in the face. All he needed was the right key to unlock the door in his mind; a word, a flashback, a memory of something odd that had occurred during the mission, but which might not have seemed so unusual at the time.

'Only a Texan could love this devil's hell-hole of a country,' sighed Dick Squires, mopping his sweaty brow and reaching for the canteen hanging from his saddle horn. His innocent observation caused Kane to nod in absent-minded agreement. A split second later, when his friend's words truly registered, he reined in, frowning.

'What's up?' queried Squires, bringing his own horse to a standstill.

Kane slapped his thigh with glee. 'You just told me who the killer is,' he said, sporting a grin as wide as the Grand Canyon.

'I did?'

Kane nodded.

'Well, are you gonna tell me who it is?'

'No,' replied Kane, shaking his head. 'Not yet. I need to get everything straight in my head first and then check on one or two things. Knowing is one thing, proving it is something else, and the one thing we'll need when we confront our murderer is evidence.'

'Will we find such in town?' asked Squires.

'Yeah,' said Kane, 'I just reckon we might at that. And when we do, we can present our case to the proper authorities and let justice run its course.'

Without further ado, the scouts kicked their mounts back into motion with a renewed sense of urgency.

They reached Miller Springs soon after midday. Their first port of call was the sheriff's office. Bates was asleep with his feet up on the battered oaken desk in front of him when the scouts entered. He came awake with a start when Kane slammed the office door shut behind him.

'What the hell!' exclaimed the lawman, jumping to his feet in a flash, his right hand reaching for the gun on his hip. 'Oh, it's you, Kane. What d'ya mean by scaring the living daylights out of me like that?' He relaxed back down into his seat.

'I thought only the Mexicans took a siesta in the middle of the day,' joked Kane, approaching the desk. He and Squires sat in the chairs directly in front of the peace officer.

'Make yourselves at home, why don't you?' offered Bates, sarcastically.

'I've hardly had time to catch my breath in more than a week,' replied Kane, toying with the battered, dusty hat he had just removed from his head. 'So I reckon to sit a spell while I tell you what's on my mind.'

'Must be something mighty important to bring you all the way out here,' said the lawman, curiosity replacing irritation. He stood up and wandered over to the stove in the corner of the small, cramped office to pour himself a cup of coffee.

'Want some?'

When the scouts nodded, he filled two more cups and carried them over to his guests before collecting his own.

'My posse failed to turn up any sign of that renegade named Curly Smith, so I hope you're here to tell me you have him penned up at the fort,' he said, returning to his seat.

Kane shook his head and then proceeded to tell Bates about everything that had happened out at the fort and during the mission to recover the stolen rifles. He kept strictly to the facts as he saw them and did not reveal his suspicions as to the identity of the killer. When he had finished his account, Kane divulged the reason behind his visit to Miller Springs. As Bates himself had failed to throw any light on the murder of the stranger, he was only too pleased to share what information he possessed in the hope of finally solving the crime.

Kane asked him a series of questions about the discovery of the body in the alleyway, all of which Bates answered to the scout's satisfaction. No unclaimed horse or other belongings had been found anywhere in Miller Springs. The few hotel guests who had been in town that day were all accounted for. The scout remained intrigued by the measures the killer had taken to make identification of the dead man all but impossible.

'The scalping was just to confuse the issue,' he insisted, 'to make it look like Curly Smith did it. But the truth is, neither Curly nor any full-blooded Comanche would bash a man's face in. That was done purely to prevent anyone from recognizing him.'

'But why bother?' queried Bates. 'If the man was a stranger in these parts, no one in Miller Springs would know him anyway.'

'The killer clearly thought otherwise,' replied Kane. 'Did the body have any distinguishing marks?'

The sheriff shrugged his shoulders. 'Nothing, save for a small birthmark just above the left elbow.'

'And he'd been stripped of everything apart from his underwear?'

Bates nodded. 'Yeah, and his long johns were almost ripped away at the neck-line.'

'Interesting,' mused Kane. 'Now, if I'm right, he must have had a very good reason for coming to town. I also reckon he arrived on the stagecoach.'

'No way,' argued the lawman. 'The stage got in after dark on the night of the killing. What few passengers there were spent the night at the hotel and then continued on their way at first light. They were all accounted for; everyone who was expected to travel that morning left on the stage; it was the first thing I checked on.'

'Then the stranger was bound for here and no place else,' insisted the scout.

Bates shook his head firmly.

'The only passenger who got off the stage that night who'd purchased a ticket only as far as Miller Springs was that dandy new captain of yours, and he rode off to the fort with his escort the very next morning.'

Kane stroked his chin thoughtfully.

'What about the two new recruits, Faraday and Jacobs? When did they arrive in town?'

'Two days before the captain,' revealed the lawman. 'Arrived on the stage with nothing more than a bedroll and the clothes they was wearing. They booked a room at Ma Peterson's guesthouse and kept themselves to themselves. I guess they heard army folk ain't any too popular around here.'

'And the troopers that were to escort the captain to the post, when did they arrive?'

Bates informed him they had ridden in at sunset on the night in question. They had enjoyed a few beers in the saloon under his watchful eye. Having satisfied himself that the regular customers, who had gathered to chew the fat or play cards, were paying them no heed, even though they resented their presence, Bates had left around ten to take his usual tour of the town before retiring to the cot in the back of his office.

'Does any of this help you make sense of what's happened?' asked the sheriff, easing himself out of his seat to replenish his empty cup.

'Yeah,' said Kane, 'it does. But I have one more question to ask. When you arrested Curly, did he seem hung over to you?'

Bates frowned as he sat down on the corner of his desk.

'Now you come to mention it, yeah he did. He

looked and moved like a man who had drunk a little too much the night before. Yet I know for a fact he never got so much as a drop to drink. Tipper refused to serve him; you know how he feels about anyone of Injun blood.'

'Curly told me he got the sergeant who commanded the escort to buy him a bottle of rot-gut from the saloon.'

'That would explain his surly mood and dull-eyed appearance,' conceded the lawman.

'It also explains how someone was able to enter the livery stable and plant the scalp in his saddle-bags without him hearing a thing. Curly was normally a light sleeper, like all us scouts. I couldn't figure out how anyone could sneak up on him like that until he told me about the whiskey bottle when I interrogated him at the mission. Then it made sense.'

'I'm still not as certain as you seem to be that Curly didn't kill the dude. What about the money we found on him?'

Kane revealed how Curly had come by the gold coins and why he had kept his mouth shut when they were discovered in his saddle-bags. His explanation convinced the sheriff of Curly's innocence. When Bates asked why the half-breed himself had been murdered, the scout suggested that the killer had not expected his stooge to escape from jail. His reappearance had presented a threat, for there was no telling what he might have remembered about the night in town.

'He opted to silence him permanently,' concluded

Kane. 'Then the killer hid his body hoping we would think Curly had made a run for it.'

'Sounds like we're up agin a right cunning bastard,' offered the lawman.

'That we are,' agreed Kane. He stood up and replaced his hat on his head. 'But he has made a couple of mistakes which put me on to him.'

'He has?'

The scout nodded.

'So you know who it is?'

'I do,' confessed Kane.

'Then why the hell didn't you say so? Why all the questions?'

'As I told my pard here,' said Kane, nodding towards a grinning Dick Squires, 'knowing's one thing, proving it's another. What you've told me certainly helps, but now I need to talk to Harry Fisher at the stage depot, or whoever else was on duty the night of the killing.'

'It was Harry,' confirmed Bates. 'But what do you think he can possibly add to what I've already told you?'

'String along with us and you'll find out!' replied Kane with a grin, heading for the door with Squires at his side.

They found the small, balding, irritable depot manager at his desk in the front office, busily working his way through a pile of routine paperwork. He didn't take too kindly to being interrupted and arrogantly insisted his visitors should wait until he had finished his task. When Kane tried politely to reason with the pompous fool, the man stubbornly continued to argue. Only when Bates informed him they were present on official sheriff's business and that he would take a dim view of any lack of co-operation did Fisher finally set his pen aside with a sigh and give them his undivided attention.

Kane asked him about the passengers who had come to town in the days leading up to the discovery of the stranger's body in the alleyway. He got him to describe them in as much detail as the depot manager could remember. When he was satisfied Fisher could offer no further information he thanked him for his help and led the way back outside into the dusty street.

'That was sure a waste of time!' exclaimed Bates. 'He didn't tell ya a thing that you didn't already know.'

'That's where you're wrong,' corrected Kane. 'He told me just what I wanted to know. I'm now more certain than ever that I know who the killer is.'

'Are you gonna share this knowledge?'

'Yeah, when the time's right.'

'So what are you aiming to do now?'

'First I'm gonna treat myself to a meal at Frenchie's restaurant, I'm absolutely ravenous, I ain't had a decent steak in a month or more.'

'Then what?' queried Bates.

'In about an hour's time the three of us are gonna take a ride out to Fort Walsh to arrest a murderer,' replied Kane.

With that, he turned his back on the sheriff and set off towards the restaurant in the middle of town. Bates looked at Squires and frowned. The scout shrugged his shoulders, grinned and set off after his friend. With a sigh and shake of his head, the young lawman fell into step behind them down the board-walk.

XV

The sun was setting in a blaze of brilliant orange by the time Kane, Squires and Bates reached the fort. On the final leg of the journey from Coyote Wells, where they had rested briefly and watered their mounts, Kane had finally revealed his hand to his companions. Although the evidence he used to mount his case was purely circumstantial, Squires and Bates were convinced he had called things right. All that remained was for them to confront the guilty party. Kane knew exactly how he wanted to proceed and sought Bates's approval for what he had in mind. For his part, the lawman was perfectly happy for the scout to play out his hand.

Having stabled their mounts, they reported directly to Major Turner. The post commander was somewhat intrigued by the sheriff's presence but Kane's explanation won his instant approval. The scout then queried whether anything else untoward had happened during his absence. He was relieved to hear that all had remained quiet.

'This is going to be tricky, Kane,' said the major.

146

'What if he simply denies everything? As you admit yourself, the evidence is purely circumstantial.'

Kane had it all figured out. His response swiftly received the Major's blessing. The redoubtable sergeant O'Reilly, the duty non-commissioned officer, was quickly summoned into the room and ordered to round up all the surviving members of the mission to Garston Crossing and have them report immediately to the enlisted mens' mess-hall.

The major waited five minutes, sufficient time to allow O'Reilly to carry out his instructions, before leading the way through the fading light across the quiet, dusty compound towards the low adobe building where the patrol had gathered. Kane warned his companions that he expected the killer to make a fight of it when he was finally exposed, so, like the lawman who walked at his side and the two scouts who brought up the rear, Turner had a loaded sidearm strapped to his waist.

All heads automatically turned towards the major's party when they entered the dimly lit messhall. Counting an irritated-looking Captain Cummings, who deeply resented being summoned from the much-needed bath he had been taking, there were ten men present in the long, rectangular room. Apart from the scowling Cummings, they were all seated along both sides of a trestle-table, close to the door. Kane and the major took up station in front of the table, where they had a clear view of the assembled troopers. Squires sauntered casually towards the far end of the room, where he stood with his back up against the wall, close to one

147

of the four oil-lamps which provided light. Bates waited patiently by the door for the fun to begin, arms casually folded across his chest, eyes watchful, as per Kane's instructions.

The silence was almost deafening. You could have cut the atmosphere with a knife. All eyes remained focused on the newcomers. The assembled troopers looked tense and fidgety. No one had any idea why they had been summoned. Kane gazed back at each of the soldiers in turn and swallowed hard. Every man present in the room, save one, averted their eyes under Kane's piercing stare. Faraday, one of the two new recruits, defiantly glared right back. Kane hoped he had called it right, otherwise he was about to make a complete fool of himself. It was Cummings who finally broke the silence.

'What is all this about, Major?' he demanded, moving casually to stand next to the open window on his side of the room. 'What are we doing here at this time of day?'

'All in good time, Captain,' replied the post commander, nodding towards the scout at his side. 'This is Kane's show, he'll explain everything.'

Cummings shook his head and sighed impatiently, while Faraday once more locked eyes with the unsmiling scout. Neither man was willing to blink or be the first to look away. Kane's bland expression gave nothing away, yet the trooper sensed bad news was coming. The guilty look which spread across his face gave the scout food for thought.

'Something on your mind, Private?' he asked.

Faraday scowled and shook his head before finally

giving up the unequal struggle. He averted his gaze to the tabletop in front of him, drumming his fingers nervously on the rough surface, much to the irritation of those seated around him. Kane was both intrigued and somewhat confused by the trooper's behaviour. However, rather than dwell upon it, he decided to press on and bring matters to a head. He surreptitiously checked that Bates and Squires were in position to respond if necessary. Satisfied his back was covered, he played his opening card.

'Someone here ain't who he claims to be,' he said, firmly but calmly.

His eyes flashed left, then right, for any trace of a reaction on the men's faces. Once again, Faraday shot him a look full of guilt and malice.

'I dare say a good few men on the post might have changed their given name for one reason or another when they enlisted, Kane,' observed Pete Flanagan. 'But you know every man jack of us, we've ridden through hell and back together, so what does it matter what a man calls himself as long as he gets the job done?'

The scout couldn't help but smile, in spite of the seriousness of the business at hand.

'So is your name really Flanagan?' he countered.

The trooper gave him a broad grin. 'It is, unless you knows different!'

'Relax, Pete,' said Kane. 'You ain't the low-down mangy cur I'm after.'

The troopers gazed at each other incredulously. A low babble of voices rose from the table as they began to engage in whispered conversations. Kane continued to run the rule over each of them in turn. Only the captain seemed unmoved by his little speech.

'Just what in Sam Hill is going on here, Sam?' asked Gimenez.

'I'm about to expose a murderer,' replied the scout. 'A no-good son of a bitch who ain't got no right to be wearing a blue uniform.'

'Damn you to hell, Kane!' roared Faraday, instantly coming to his feet. He leapt across the table and threw himself at the scout.

Kane, caught unawares, was sent flying heavily into the adobe wall at his back. The speed and ferocity of the charge knocked the wind out of him, but he still managed somehow to remain on his feet. The combatants desperately grappled to gain the upper hand in the confined space between the wall and the table. Suddenly, a loud explosion reverberated around the room. Faraday grunted loudly, put a hand to his lower left back, and fell to his knees in front of the astonished scout.

The stink of sulphur powder permeated the mess-hall. Kane looked up from the mortally wounded trooper to find himself staring into the smoking barrel of Captain Cummings' Navy Colt. Nobody else had moved a muscle. They were transfixed, like statues carved from marble.

'Put your gun away, Captain,' said Kane, firmly.

'Is that all the thanks I get?' demanded Cummings, standing his ground. 'He might have killed you if I hadn't shot him.'

'I doubt that,' corrected Kane. 'Now do as I say

and put that damn gun back in its holster, right now!'

'I'd do jest like the man says,' warned Dick Squires, keeping his own trusty six-shooter trained on the disgruntled officer's midriff. 'I'd sure hate to have to plug you where you stand.'

The captain was fit to be tied, but he did as he was told with an angry scowl and a loud, 'humph', thrown in for good measure. He stood leaning back against the wall with his arms folded moodily across his chest.

Kane dropped to his knees in front of the stricken trooper. Faraday coughed violently twice, bringing up blood each time. He slowly raised his head to stare into the scout's puzzled face through watery eyes. A sharp spasm of pain in the region of his mangled kidney made him double over again. Blood flowed ever more freely from the corner of his mouth as he lifted his head once more. He coughed again.

'How did you know?' he queried, his breathless words barely audible through his pain. 'How did you know I was wanted for killing that fella up in Kansas?'

Before Kane had a chance to answer for himself, the dying trooper did so for him.

'I guess the sheriff must have had a Wanted poster on me. I was hoping they wouldn't be looking for me down here in Texas.'

'What's your real name, fella?' called an intrigued Bates from the door.

'Vince Deacon,' wheezed the trooper they knew as Faraday.

'Never heard of ya!' exclaimed the lawman, impassively. 'Ain't carrying no poster on anyone of that name.'

'Jest my luck,' coughed Deacon, his eyes glazing over. He fought to catch his breath, then toppled over on to his side. Kane looked at Bates and shook his head.

'He's a gonner,' he advised, coming to his feet. The scout swiftly turned to face Captain Cummings. 'That's the third time you've taken a shot at me, and the third time you've missed!'

'What are you saying?' roared Cummings, his face red with rage. 'You're mad!'

'Well, one of us sure is!' conceded Kane.

'I shot him to save your life.'

The scout shook his head.

'Why on earth would I want to kill you?'

'Now that's an interesting question, and one that took me a while to fathom out. I just couldn't see what motive you might have had for killing me or the others on your death list.'

'What others?'

'The man in town was the first, then Rothwell, York, Curly Smith, young Gannon and, finally, Halliday.'

'But for Christ sakes, how can you say such a thing?' argued Cummings. 'It's common knowledge on the post that Halliday killed Rothwell, York, Smith and Gannon, then committed suicide having been caught red-handed trying to kill you.'

'Halliday didn't kill anyone, nor did he take his own life,' stated Kane, much to the other troopers' surprise. 'You're the one who murdered them all.'

'No!' insisted Cummings, angrily. 'If Halliday wasn't the murderer, then Faraday, or whatever his real name was, must be. After all, you just heard him 'fess up to being a killer!'

'Oh, our dead friend was a killer all right,' agreed the scout. 'I don't doubt for a moment he killed a man in Kansas. He thought I'd found out about it, which is why he panicked and came after me. In the confusion you saw your chance to finally plug me, and you might have too, if'n the unfortunate trooper hadn't inadvertently stepped right in front of me at the vital second.'

'You've taken leave of your senses, scout!' raged the captain.

'Not at all,' insisted Kane. 'You're guilty and I can prove it.'

The captain's beady eyes darted about the room. Squires and Bates steadfastly stood their ground, gun in hand, happy to support Kane from their respective corners of the room.

'OK then,' offered Cummings. 'You say you can prove it, so go right ahead. I'd like to hear what you have to say.'

Kane started off by listing the circumstantial evidence against the captain; the killings had only started after he arrived at the post; he was present when all the victims met their fate; and he had every opportunity to carry out the crimes. Cummings immediately countered by reminding everyone that the same could have been said about Faraday, or Jacobs come to that. Kane was forced to concede the point, but he soon removed the smug look on

Cummings' face by informing his highly attentive audience that the captain had also made two serious mistakes, the first in town, when he killed the man in the alleyway, and the second while leading the patrol sent out to recover the stolen rifles from the Comancheros.

'And what mistakes would they be?' scoffed Cummings, rubbing his neck where the collar of his tunic was chaffing his skin. The major instantly noticed his discomfort.

'After you ambushed the man in town, you should have stripped him naked instead of leaving him in his long johns,' said Kane. 'When the sheriff mentioned the tear in the neckline of the victim's underwear it got me to thinking that maybe the killer had ripped the label out of the material for some reason. Then I figured out what it might be. All cavalry-issue underwear carries a US army mark. I put two and two together and reasoned that the body had to be that of a cavalryman. Now the only cavalryman who arrived in town on the night in question was Captain Cummings, which means you must have killed him in order to steal his identity.'

'Please tell me you don't believe any of this horse-shit, Major?' pleaded Cummings, desperately trying to maintain his innocence. Turner stared him right in the eyes.

'Oh but I most certainly do,' he assured him, calmly. 'For one thing, it might help to explain why your tunic doesn't appear to fit you quite right. A bit tight around the neck I reckon.'

'This is all nonsense!' maintained Cummings, his

face turning puce with rage.

'No it ain't,' replied Kane. 'But if you hadn't panicked when the Comanches were hot on our tail and made your second big mistake I might never have found you out.'

'So what did I do?' sneered the accused, haughtily.

'It was you who suggested we should seek cover in the abandoned mission.'

'So what?'

'I didn't think of it at the time, I guess I was too busy trying to figure out a way to save our hides, but only someone who knew the territory real well would have known about the mission, and yet you told me when we left Debbie's ranch that this was your first time in Texas.'

'You must have misheard me,' replied an increasingly flustered-looking Cummings. 'I clearly remember revealing that I'd spent some time here prior to the War between the States.'

'You're a damned liar!' snorted Kane.

Cummings shrugged his shoulders. 'None of this will stand up in court,' he insisted. 'You can't prove a thing.'

'We will,' stated Major Turner, 'when we get someone out here who knew the real Captain Cummings. Then we'll have all the confirmation we need that you're an impostor.'

Cummings smiled, then slowly shook his head. He made to speak, then spun adroitly on his heels to dive out through the open window. Bates bolted out of the door after him, with Kane and Squires hot on his tail.

The darkness had instantly swallowed their quarry. There was no sign of him anywhere. As Major Turner joined them out in the parade ground, Kane suggested they split up to cover the compound. He set off in the direction of the stables and corral, leaving the others to search the rest of the buildings on the post.

The dark shapes in the corral paid him no heed as he passed by *en route* to the Judas gate in the main door of the stables. He found it slightly ajar. Having drawn his gun, he eased his way inside the pitch-black, musty interior of the building, keeping low. A bullet instantly nicked the top of his hat. He dived behind a pile of hay bales directly in front of him, from where he returned fire. Two more shots in quick succession sent dust and hay spinning into the air as he squatted down behind his makeshift barricade.

'Give it up!' he yelled, 'there ain't but one way out of here, you've nowhere left to run.'

'Never,' came the reply from somewhere in the deep, dark recesses of the stable. 'Leastways, not 'til I see you in hell!'

Two more bullets quickly slammed into the wall at Kane's back. The scout swallowed hard and then rolled sideways along the ground towards the corner of the building. His quarry must have sensed which way he was heading, for another shot caught him in the left shoulder, just short of the water barrel he was intending to use for cover. He slowly climbed to his feet, gritting his teeth against the burning, debilitating pain in his shoulder.

THE FIRST TO DIE

'As I recall, you only had your Navy Colt with you in the mess-hall,' he stated, steadying himself on his firmly planted feet. 'And as I've counted six shots, I reckon you're out of ammunition, my friend.'

With a loud roar, the man he knew as Cummings charged out of the darkness, like an enraged bull. Almost too late, Kane sensed the fugitive had something long and lethal in his outstretched hands. The innermost point of the extended pitchfork tore through his blood-soaked shirt, just missing flesh. Before his assailant could withdraw the weapon for another try, Kane swung the Colt clenched tightly in his right hand to catch him a glancing blow to the side of the head. The man let go of the pitchfork and collapsed to his knees with a loud grunt.

Kane pulled the pitchfork clear of his shredded shirt, casually discarding it as he stepped forward to confront the fallen figure kneeling before him. The sound of running feet heralded the arrival of Turner, Squires, Bates and a number of interested troopers.

'Find a lamp,' instructed the major.

One of the soldiers instantly obeyed. Shadows danced eerily on the walls of the stables as Squires examined the wound in his friend's shoulder, while the bemused troopers kept the moaning fugitive, whom Bates had just hauled to his feet, covered with their pistols.

'Must hurt some,' he offered with a wry grin.

'It do,' conceded Kane. He looked Cummings in the eye. Blood oozed out from between the man's fingers as he tightly gripped his split left ear. 'Just who the hell are you?'

'Ain't you figured it out yet, scout?' snarled the fugitive.

Kane shook his head.

'My name is Jacob Harmer. You damn Yankees murdered my young son, and my brother.'

'You're Tom Harmer's brother?' asked an incredulous Bates.

'Yeah,' he snarled. 'And I almost managed to settle the score for my son and Tom. I killed everyone of those yellow-bellied soldiers who were involved. You're the only one left, Kane. I knew I should have killed you first.'

'You sure tried hard enough!' quipped the scout, wincing with pain when he moved his damaged shoulder a mite too quickly for comfort. 'But why kill Rothwell? He had nothing to do with the death of your son or brother.'

'He recognized me when I arrived at the post. We knew each other back in Missouri before the war. I had to kill him before he gave me away.'

Kane nodded. 'I guess that ties up all the loose ends.'

'Take Mr Harmer to the guardhouse,' instructed the major. A pair of privates duly obliged. 'We'll provide you with an escort for your prisoner when you take him to town in the morning, sheriff.'

Bates expressed his gratitude for the offer as the assembled company strolled out into the still, humid, night air.

An hour after sun-up, the sheriff, four troopers and their heavily shackled prisoner were mounted and ready to ride. Kane, arm in a sling, came to meet them as they set off from the guardhouse. Bates reined in and reached down to shake hands with the scout.

'I'll be paying a call on Tom Harmer's widow once I've got my prisoner safely locked up,' he said. 'I reckon we can prove she was a part of all this.'

Kane nodded. 'At the very least she must have hidden him at her house when he arrived in town,' he said. 'That's why no one had seen him before he showed up in uniform.'

'Be seeing you, Kane,' said Bates, spurring his mount into motion.

Kane sighed deeply as he watched the riders disappear into the shimmering early-morning heat, glad that an air of normality had at last returned to the post. One man's hate had led to the deaths of six innocent souls. Now the troopers of Fort Walsh could go about their duties without nervously looking back over their shoulders. No, from now on, all they had to worry about were Comanches, Comancheros and border outlaws. Normality indeed!